I0615519

Ezra Ferris

The early settlement of the Miami Country

Ezra Ferris

The early settlement of the Miami Country

ISBN/EAN: 9783742825193

Manufactured in Europe, USA, Canada, Australia, Japa

Cover: Foto ©Andreas Hilbeck / pixelio.de

Manufactured and distributed by brebook publishing software
(www.brebook.com)

Ezra Ferris

The early settlement of the Miami Country

INDIANA HISTORICAL SOCIETY PUBLICATIONS.

VOLUME I   NUMBER IX

THE EARLY SETTLEMENT

OF THE

MIAMI COUNTRY

BY

DR. EZRA FERRIS

INDIANAPOLIS
THE BOWEN-MERRILL COMPANY
1897

(243)

PREFACE.

The following letters were not originally written for the Indiana Historical Society, or printed by it, but it is deemed proper to publish them in connection with the earlier work of the Society because the author, Dr. Ezra Ferris, was a charter member of the Society, and the editor, Oliver B. Torbet, who induced him to write them, was also a member. The *Independent Press*, of Lawrenceburg, Ind., was started in the fall of 1850, the first number appearing on October 18, of that year. The proprietors, Henry L. Brown and James E. Goble, attended to the mechanical and business departments, and employed Mr. Torbet to conduct the editorial department. Mr. Torbet was ambitious to make the paper popular, and wisely undertook to secure a series of historical articles from Dr. Ferris, who was acknowledged on all sides to know more of the early history of that region than any other person. As the *Press* was a Whig paper, and Dr. Ferris was a very earnest Whig, the arrangement was speedily made, and the first article was ready for the *Press* on December 12, 1850. The paper was sold to Rev. W. W. Hibben on August 22, 1851, but the letters were continued for some time afterwards, as appears by their dates.

Dr. Ezra Ferris was born at Stanwich, Conn., April 26, 1783. When he was six years old his parents emigrated to the wilderness north of the Ohio river, and his account of the trip and the subsequent life at Columbia forms a part of the following letters. Among the pioneers at that point were a

(245)

number of others, who afterwards settled in southeastern Indiana, so that his account of the experiences of the pioneers who were cooped up there is doubly a chapter in Indiana history.   Dr. Ferris, as a boy, had the benefit of some schooling at Columbia, and it is said that later he attended a school in the East.   When quite a young man he was licensed as a preacher at the Duck Creek Baptist Church, and was afterwards ordained as an elder.   For several years he taught school at Lebanon, Ohio, and, during his work in other lines, he studied medicine.   Later he removed to Lawrenceburg, where he practiced medicine, and also established a drugstore, which has been continued by his descendants to this day.   He was elected a member of the constitutional convention when Indiana was admitted as a state, and in that body served as chairman of the committee on the elective franchise and on elections.   Later he was elected to the legislature.   When the state government was organized, he was elected by the legislature one of the censors for licensing physicians in the third medical district.   In politics he was a Whig, so long as the Whig party lasted, and was always an earnest advocate of his political faith.

Much of the time and talent of Dr. Ferris were devoted to religious work.   The Baptist churches of southeastern Indiana were poor, and, as a consistent advocate of ''a free gospel,'' he preached, without compensation, throughout his life, to the congregation at Lawrenceburg, as well as at odd times to the one at Salem, and to some others of the vicinity.   An incident in the local church history illustrates the peculiar tact and shrewdness of the man.   It was at the time when the doctrines of Alexander Campbell were attracting many members of the Baptist church, and many congregations were going over bodily to the new organization.   An agent of the Disciples appeared at Lawrenceburg and found several of the Baptists favorably disposed.   A meeting was appointed, at which the proposition of going over as a congregation was to be submitted. Dr. Ferris was not taken into the confidence of the movers, but he learned what was going on and appeared at the meeting and took charge of it by virtue of his official position as calmly as if it were one of the stated meetings of the church. The members of the other faction were somewhat startled by this, but imagine their feelings when he arose and opened the meeting by reading Charles Wesley's hymn:

> Jesus, great Shepherd of the sheep,
>   To thee for help we fly;
> Thy little flock in safety keep,
>   For Oh! the wolf is nigh.
>
> He comes, of hellish malice full,
>   To scatter, tear and slay;
> He seizes every straggling soul
>   As his own lawful prey.
>
> Us into thy protection take,
>   And gather with thine arm;
> Unless the fold we first forsake,
>   The wolf can never harm.
>
> We laugh to scorn his cruel power,
>   While by our Shepherd's side;
> The sheep he never can devour,
>   Unless he first divide.
>
> O do not suffer him to part
>   The souls that here agree;
> But make us of one mind and heart,
>   And keep us one in thee.
>
> Together let us sweetly live—
>   Together let us die;
> And each a starry crown receive,
>   And reign above the sky.

When this had been sung he delivered a brief but earnest petition for divine protection from discord or dissension, for freedom from temptation to leave the straight and narrow path, for deliverance from any and all evils that might threaten them. Then he announced that the visiting brother would address the meeting. But the visiting brother was unnerved. He talked for a while, but did not introduce the contemplated subject at all. The meeting was dismissed with the benediction, and the Lawrenceburg church remained in the Baptist fold.

With all his earnestness in political and religious matters Dr. Ferris held the universal esteem and respect of his fellowcitizens. He was a useful member of society, always lending a hand to beneficial movements in the community. After middle life he retired from the practice of his profession, but continued his drug store to the time of his death, April 19, 1857.

THE EARLY SETTLEMENT OF THE MIAMI COUNTRY.

LETTER I.

MR. TORBET—In compliance with your request, I send you the following account of my first settlement in the Miami country: A short time before my father started on his journey to the west, and after he had determined to do so, a sermon was preached at his house on the occasion, from Genesis xii : 1 : "Now the Lord said unto Abraham, get thee out of thy country and from thy kindred, and from thy father's house, unto a land that I will shew thee." On the 20th of September, 1789, according to previous arrangement, my father, in company with his own and two other families, left his native village (Stanwich, in the state of Connecticut), and separated himself and family from all the associations and endearing ties which had been formed during the life of fifty years, to seek for himself and them a home in the then western wilderness. Though I was a boy of only six years of age, I have a very distinct and vivid recollection of the affecting occasion. The enterprise at that time was so novel and daring it drew together a vast crowd of people to witness the parting scene. When, for the last time, the family left the house, and bid farewell to relatives and neighbors, it was an affecting scene; what added poignancy to their grief was, that their separation would be, probably, while on earth, final. As they took their seats in

(249)

the wagon, and moved down the road, they were surrounded by a crowd on every side; many of whom were heard to predict the result of so hazardous a journey. Some feared they would fall a sacrifice to savage cruelty, others thought they would all be drowned in descending the western rivers. But nothing could overcome the dauntless courage of this little company; and they passed down the road on the north side of Long Island Sound to the city of New York, whence they passed over into New Jersey—traveled through that state and Pennsylvania over the Alleghany mountains, until they came to the waters of the Youghiogheny, thence down the river to the Monongahela, and down that river to Pittsburg, thence down the Ohio to Ft. Miami, about three-fourths of a mile below the Little Miami, at which place they arrived on the 12th day of December, 1789, just sixty-one years past; having been two months and twenty days on the journey, thankful to kind Providence, who had preserved them in all dangers through which they had passed, and that at last they had reached their intended future home, where they could enjoy the rest they so much needed after the fatigues of the journey of one thousand miles. In approaching the shore they were met by a crowd of smiling faces, to bid them a hearty welcome, and offer them all the assistance circumstances would admit of. An apartment in the fort (of about sixteen feet square) was assigned each family, in which, for the time, they resided. Ft. Miami consisted of four long rows of buildings in the form of an oblong, or, rather, four long buildings, for they were all connected together, but divided into different apartments, with a block-house at each corner, projecting a few feet beyond the range of other buildings, so that no Indian could approach any part in the ring without exposing himself to the fire of the white people from the block-houses. Here were found collected together some thirty or more families living in this fort, without the restraints of civil law, destitute of all kinds of provisions, except what they could obtain from the woods, surrounded by a vast (and to the white man) un-explored forest, filled with numerous tribes of hostile savages, without manufactories, or even the common work-shops of the mechanic, such as the blacksmith or the shoemaker, with-out houses, barns or fields, save those that were covered over with forest trees, without a physician for the sick or gospel minister to try to comfort them when dying. They soon learned the repose to be indulged in here was but temporary. Much was to be done to provide for coming wants, and that must be done in the face of great danger. Excessive labor must be performed to clear, fence and cultivate the ground, so as to secure a crop of corn, which was their principal object; for as yet no crop had been raised in the country so as to ripen. The difficulties, however, were all overcome, and, by continued train of exertion, the face of the country has been changed from what I then saw it to what it is now. In look-ing back to the beginning, and tracing the progress of the improvement of the country from that time to the present, I am ready to inquire, who dare to undertake to prescribe bounds to what human industry and enterprise may accomplish?

Lawrenceburg, Ind., Dec. 12, 1850. E. F.

LETTER II.

MR. TORBET — An observing mind, made acquainted with the circumstances surrounding the infant settlement at Fort Miami, as described in my letter of the 12th inst., would naturally be led to inquire, what motives could have prompted the inhabitants of that place to venture so far in advance of other frontier settlements, and expose themselves to such imminent danger. Such an inquiry suggested itself to my mind, and being personally acquainted with nearly every individual comprising the party who made the first landing to remain as permanent residents of the country, I instituted the inquiry of persons who I supposed had the best opportunity of knowing, which resulted in the following statement of facts, which I submitted to the inspection of several of the same party, after they were penned, who pronounced the whole, so far as it went, to be correct:

Major Benjamin Stites, the pioneer of this company, was a native of Scotch Plains, Essex county, New Jersey, but when young emigrated to western Pennsylvania and settled on Ten Mile Creek, within the bounds of what is now Green county. In the spring of the year 1787, he descended the Ohio river in a flat-boat loaded with castings, flour, whisky, etc., to Limestone (now Maysville), Ky., in pursuit of a market; but after staying there a few days, with but little success, he removed a few miles back from the river to Washington, the county seat of Mason county, where there was a prospect of better sales. One night, while at the latter place, the Indians committed hostilities on the inhabitants of the vicinity by stealing and taking off a number of horses. The next morning a number of militia volunteered to pursue after the Indians and try to recapture the horses and punish the aggressors. Major Stites, who possessed extraordinary physical powers and undaunted courage, volunteered to accompany them. Necessary preparations being made, they commenced the pursuit, following the trail of the horses on the Kentucky side down the Ohio river, a short distance below the mouth of the Little Miami river, to a place where the Indians had crossed the Ohio river with the horses, on a raft. Determined to continue the pursuit, the white men adopted the same plan of crossing the river, and pursued the Indians up the valley of the Miami nearly to an Indian village called Old

Chillicothe, near the headwaters of the Little Miami, but without success. On their return, passing down between the two Miamis, they had a good opportunity to examine the country. Major Stites was so well pleased with the face of the country and the fertility of the soil, that he determined, before recrossing the river, to attempt to make a settlement at the mouth of the Little Miami. After his return to Washington, he closed his business there as speedily as possible, and returned to his family to make the necessary arrangements to enable him to accomplish his object. He stayed a short time with them, then crossed the mountains to visit his native state to try to procure means and men to accompany him, so as to be able to prosecute his previous designs. On his arrival at Trenton, N. J., he had an introduction to the late Judge John C. Symmes, to whom he related the discovery he had made, and the object of his visit to New Jersey. From Judge Symmes he learned, for the first time, that the country northwest of the Ohio belonged to the United States, and that a legal title for the land could only be obtained from congress. Judge Symmes proposed to join in the enterprise to which Major Stites consented. It was then agreed that, as congress was about to assemble at Philadelphia, Judge Symmes (who was a member from New Jersey) should make an application for the purchase of the land, and that Stites should prosecute his journey to raise men to accompany him if Symmes should be successful. It was also agreed, if successful, that Stites, for the discovery, should have ten thousand acres of land at the mouth of the Little Miami, to be laid off as nearly in a square as the nature of the case would admit of, and as much more as he could pay for.

Judge Symmes succeeded in purchasing one million acres, to include all the land lying on the Ohio, between the two Miamis, running back for quantity, congress reserving three sections in each township, viz.: One for the support of schools, one for the support of the gospel, and one for future sale, and in like manner one entire township to support a university; the whole to be laid off in townships six miles square, and sections one mile square, each section to be sub-divided into four equal parts.

Major Stites also succeeded in raising a number of men to accompany him, and in making arrangements to prosecute the journey to his intended new home. Previous to making any sales of land they published the conditions of settling the Miami country in a very small pamphlet, printed at Trenton; one of which conditions was that each tract of land sold and not settled on by the purchaser within three years should be subject to a forfeiture of one-sixth part. For the benefit of any male person who was not the owner of land in the country, and who would enter upon it, and raise a log cabin, and clear and cultivate three acres of land three years, such persons should be entitled to a deed for the same, thus presenting to emigrants, without other means, the prospect of acquiring land in the new settlement. It was further agreed to assemble their forces on the western waters and descend the Ohio river to Maysville, at as early a period as practicable, preparatory to taking possession of their newly acquired lands, which shall be the subject of my next letter.   E. F.

Lawrenceburg, Ind., Dec. 27, 1850.

LETTER III.

MR. TORBET—The parties of which I wrote in my letter of the 26th, having assembled their forces at Maysville and Washington, Ky., preparatory to taking possession of their newly acquired lands, thought it most prudent to raise a company of volunteer militia to go in advance of their families, and make a further examination of the country. This company consisted of about sixty men, who descended the Ohio to the mouth of the Big Miami in the month of August, 1788, and explored the country some distance back from that place and North Bend. While at the latter place one of the company who had gone out with a small hunting party in search of game was killed by the Indians near the place where the town of Cleves now stands. After making the necessary examination, and after Judge Symmes had determined to locate his party at North Bend, they meandered along the Ohio river, measuring the distance along the beach from the Big to the Little Miami, and returned to Maysville. During the absence of this party Major Stites, who stayed behind for that purpose, was employed in preparing to remove with his company to the mouth of the Little Miami. He fixed on a plan for a fort, and that it might be built with as little delay as possible, he and his son, Benjamin Stites, with others in his employ, went to the woods and made a large quantity of clap-boards, which they hauled to the river and put in a boat; they also took with them the heart pieces of the timber, to be used in filling the open spaces between the logs of their cabin, they also made double plank doors with hangings attached so as to be able to prepare for defense as speedily as possible if attacked. In returning from the woods one evening, while engaged in making these preparations, Nehemiah Stites, a youth who had accompanied them, and who was a nephew of Major Stites, was killed by the Indians.

All things being ready, Major Stites, with the families who were to settle with him, left Maysville on the 17th of November, 1788, to descend the river to the mouth of the Little Miami. (Judge Symmes had to tarry behind a few days to await the arrival of some provisions on the way down the river.) This company consisted of Major Benjamin Stites and family, Elijah Stites and family, Groenbright Bayley and

family, Abel Cook and family and Jacob Mills and family.
They were also accompanied by Hezekiah Stites, John S,
Gano, Ephraim Kibbey, Thomas C. Wade, Elijah Mills, Ed-
mond Buxton, Daniel Shoemaker, Mr. Heampsted, Evan
Shelby, Allen Woodruff, Joseph Cox and Benjamin Cox,
without families, and there were in the family of Major Stites,
Benjamin Stites, Jr., and Jonathan Stites, and in the family of
Mr. Bayley, James F. Bayley and Reason Bayley, who were
young men, making in all twenty-two male persons able to
perform the labor and act the part in defense of men. To
take advantage of the cover of the night and to have a full
day before them when they should arrive they landed at
Bracken (now Augusta, Ky.,) and stayed until there would,
in their judgment, be about time to float down to the Little
Miami about daylight. Previous to leaving Maysville they
had heard a report that some hunters had returned from a
hunting tour who had seen five hundred Indians at the mouth
of the Little Miami who heard that the white people were
coming there to settle, and were waiting there to kill them as
soon as they should land. On approaching the place of their
destination about daybreak some of the females were very
much alarmed on account of the report alluded to. To allay
their fears five men volunteered their service to go in advance
of the boats in a canoe. If they found Indians they were to
pass on and join the boats below, if not they were to wave
their handkerchiefs as a token for the boats to land. No Indians having been discovered, they gave the token for the
boats to land, which by that time were nearly opposite the
mouth of the Miami, and close to the Kentucky shore. As
soon as could be, after the signal was given the boats were
landed, but in rowing across the Ohio river were carried by
the current about three-fourths of a mile down the river, and
made a landing on the first high bank on the Ohio below the
mouth of the Miami, a little after sunrise on the 18th of

November, 1788. After making their boats fast they ascended the steep bank and cleared a small space of ground in the midst of a papaw thicket. They then placed sentinels out to watch for the approach of Indians, and commenced a season of worship and thanksgiving to Almighty God, to whose providence they ascribed their success; first in a song of praise in which Mr. Wade took the lead, then in prayer upon their bended knees, in which Major Stites led, returning their thanks for the care exercised over them and in humble prayer imploring that protection which God alone could afford them.   E. F.

Lawrenceburg, Dec. 30, 1850.

LETTER IV.

Mr. Torbet—To avoid spinning out my last letter to too great a length, I broke off rather abruptly, leaving the little company of whom I was writing at the close of their morning worship. That exercise having closed, they commenced building Ft. Miami, as described in my first letter, and so successful were they, that before the usual hour of retirement they had erected the body of a block-house, hung the door and stopped the cracks between the logs, so as to have a place of defense to rest in. It being considered by them very important to finish their fort before the Indians should learn they were there, they persevered in their labor from day to day until it was completed, which was in about one month from their first landing, during all of which time they were careful to keep sentinels to give an alarm if the Indians should appear. The work being completed, they announced the event in military style, by firing a few rounds,

17

using on the occasion their rifles and a brass blunderbuss with which Judge Symmes had kindly furnished them when they left Maysville. There were at the time some hunters on the Kentucky side of the river who heard the firing, and, supposing the Indians had attacked the new settlement, they returned with all possible speed to Washington to give the alarm, and in less than forty-eight hours from the firing, the company at the fort were surprised to see over fifty brave, generous-hearted Kentuckians come to their relief; among them, the celebrated Indian hunter, Major Simon Kenton. Though they did not need assistance at that time, it was a source of encouragement to know the willingness of their Kentucky friends to assist them if they should afterwards want help. They received them with heartfelt gratitude, which was increased to overflowing when they left, on hearing the assurance they gave, to hold themselves in readiness to respond to any call for help they might afterwards make on them. The fort being finished, and the best preparations made for defense they were able to make, not having seen any Indians, and being greatly encouraged by the arrival of Lieutenant (afterward general) Kingsbury, of the U. S. army, with a small company of soldiers, they began to think of making preparations to raise a crop of corn the ensuing season. For that purpose they appointed three of their company to select land which could be prepared for planting with the least amount of labor. The men then appointed selected an open piece of land up the Miami about one mile from the fort, which they called "Turkey Bottom," on account of the great number of turkeys seen there. On the land selected by them there was but little timber, except honey-locust, which easily deadened, the balance being mostly hackberry and box-elder, with a few very large sycamore, which they kept at a distance from in laying out their corn-fields. On their return to the fort, they unexpectedly found themselves in the midst of a party of Indians, superior in number to themselves, to whom they had so nearly approached that there was no chance for retreat. Mr. Heampsted raised his rifle, placing his finger on the trigger, and was in the attitude of shooting one of the Indians (Capt. Black Fish), when the latter threw the muzzle of the gun above his head, saying, "Do not shoot, I'm your friend." Ascertaining that one of the Indians could speak English, and that they were disposed to be friendly, they entered into a conversation with them about their new settlement and the advantages both parties might derive in the way of trade with each other from living near together. The Indians then proposed to go with the white men to the fort to see the white people, to which they consented, on condition that one white man and one Indian should first go into the fort and give notice that they were coming, and obtain consent of the white people. The other two white men were to remain with the Indians as a guarantee that the Indian going to the fort should be permitted to return unhurt. To this proposition both parties agreed, and one of each went into the fort and obtained permission for the Indians to make the desired visit, provided they would come in unarmed, so as not to alarm the women. On receiving the information they all proceeded to the fort, leaving their guns, tomahawks, etc., behind. After spending some time in friendly conversation, the Indians returned, both parties giving mutual pledges of friendship. The Indians, on leaving, invited the white people to visit them next day at their camp, east of the Little Miami, near the place where New Town now stands. The next morning Messrs. Ephraim Kibbey and Hezekiah Stites rode out to their camp, when they found about thirty Indians, including squaws and children, encamped for a winter's hunt, who gave them a very friendly reception. Kibbey and Stites were soon invited by two Indians to spend the day in hunting, to which they consented, and soon left camp for the woods, dividing

into two parties, Kibbey going with one Indian and Stites with
the other. The day proved unfavorable for hunting, so that
they killed but one buck, though they remained in the woods
until it was too late to return to the fort that night, and were
compelled to remain with the Indians, in their camp, until
the next morning, where, for fear of wearying the reader with
too long a letter, I shall leave them until my next.

Yours truly,   E. F.

Lawrenceburg, Ind., Jan. 10, 1851.

LETTER V.

MR. TORBET—I will now proceed with my narrative of
the adventure of Messrs. Kibbey and Stites to the Indian
camp. After their return from the woods the Indians provided them with as good a supper as circumstances would admit of, and, after eating, laid skins on the ground for a bed
to sleep; so that they enjoyed a pretty good night's rest, and
in the morning in like manner prepared for them a good,
wholesome breakfast. After eating they saddled their horses
to return to the fort, when the Indian who hunted with Kibbey the day before offered him all the meat he had killed;
Kibbey, through modesty, at first refused to accept, but being told by one of them who could speak English that Indians always considered it unfriendly to refuse an offered
gift, he accepted the offer and tied it across his saddle. On
noticing this transaction the Indian who hunted with Stites
went back of the camp and selected from some venison he
had previously killed an equal quantity and presented it to
him, which he thankfully received. They then invited the
Indians to visit them again at the fort, and to bring their
women and children with them, which they promised to do,

then bid them good-bye and returned to the fort. On their return the white people were greatly rejoiced, for they had, through the night entertained strong doubts about their safety. The next day the Indians came in with their women and children, were treated very kindly, and appeared much pleased with the friendly interview. The women amused themselves with many curiosities they saw about the fort, but nothing seemed to attract their attention so much as an infant child (daughter of Mrs. Rhoda Stites, wife of Elijah Stites,) two or three days old, called Jane (after marriage Jane Blue) and the first white child born in the Miami country. After remaining a few hours in the fort, in which they appeared to enjoy their visit, they began to make preparations to return to their camp, when Major Stites told them in a few days it would be Christmas, a day generally observed as a holy day by the white people, and invited them to come in and partake of a Christmas dinner with them, to which they assented, then bid them good-bye and retired. About this time the new settlers were encouraged by the arrival of several families who had descended the river to join them; among the families was Mr. Hugh Dunn, from New Jersey. Mr. Dunn had in his family two sons, Micajah and Samuel, and a nephew, Samuel Dunn, who were active young men, besides several younger children, among whom were Elizabeth, now Mrs. Elizabeth Mills, of Elizabethtown, Ohio, and Judge Isaac Dunn, of Lawrenceburg, Ind., who still enjoys good health and is active in his business pursuits. On the approach of Christmas, preparation was made to entertain the Indians with a suitable dinner, to which Lieutenant Kingsbury and his men were invited. The dinner consisted of a turkey pot-pie, cooked in two large pot-metal kettles, over a fire made by the side of a large sycamore tree which had been cut down outside of the fort, and a table was made in the late Kentucky barbecue style. The Indians came in, and everything moved on quietly until the dinner was made ready. When about to sit down at the table Kingsbury with his soldiers made their appearance, of which the Indians had not been apprised, and on their near approach, seeing them armed, some of the Indians, fearing it was a hostile move, became alarmed, and one of them giving a sign by whistling on his fingers, they started to run, but Major Stites by calling to them and assuring them that nothing unfriendly was intended, they returned and partook of the dinner prepared for them, well pleased, but could not account for the hot pungent taste of the pot-pie. From that time the Indians and white people kept up almost a daily friendly intercourse, until the former left in the spring to return to their village to prepare for a summer crop, but on leaving they stole and took away with them what few horses the white people had, which was at that time a severe loss.

During the remainder of the holidays there was but little for the white people to do but to amuse themselves in the best way they could, as a swell in the river cut off their communication with the woods and confined them to a very narrow circle around the fort. Unfortunately Lieutenant Kingsbury had selected too low a site for his fort, and was by this flood driven from his position. As all his begun works were submerged he immediately loosed his cable in search of a more suitable place, which he did not find until he passed the mouth of Deer creek, where he made a landing, immediately above the foot of Broadway, where the next day he commenced building a fort as near the bluff bank as he could place it, and in front of the site where Fort Washington was afterwards erected. This was known for several years as the Picket fort, and was used as a prison in which the captive Indians brought in by Generals Wilkinson and Scott in 1790 were confined. Mr. Hezekiah Stites, from whom I received the information of Kingsbury's removal from Columbia to

Cincinnati, and who accompanied him to the latter place, stated to me many years ago that it took place on the last day of December, 1788, and that then no previous improvements had been commenced in Cincinnati. This brings me to the close of the year, and so I conclude this letter that my next may begin with the new year.

Yours truly,   E. F.

Published Jan. 17, 1851.

LETTER VI.

MR. TORBET—The year 1781 commenced with prospects more encouraging to the new settlement than had been anticipated; the dread of Indian hostilities had partially subsided, and though there was a scarcity of bread, deer, bear, turkeys and other wild game furnished an abundant supply of meat, and hickory and beech nuts could be had in any quantity wanted, at any time, by picking them up. Under the pleasing prospects before them the settlers commenced making preparations in Turkey-bottom to plant a crop of corn. In the meantime their numbers were increasing by the arrival of new emigrants; not only to strengthen but to establish two new settlements, one opposite the mouth of Licking river (now called Cincinnati), the other at North Bend. Among those who remained at Columbia were several families of the Flinns, one a very aged man, said to be ninety, with three sons, Thomas, Daniel and James; the two former had families, and were all good woodsmen. Other families soon followed, viz.: Captain Benjamin Davis, Mr. Newel, several families of the Clawsons, Biddles, Fletchers, Covalts, Gerrards, a Mr. Soward, and three young men without families, Luke, Gabriel and Zebulon Foster; Luke afterwards Judge

Foster, still resides on his farm in Springfield township, Hamilton county, Ohio, at an advanced age. All the above named persons arrived in time to assist in the preparations made for a crop. The arrangement among themselves was for each man to determine for himself the quantity of land he would clear, the whole to be enclosed in one common field, each one to make his proper proportion of fence. In prosecuting their work they were unexpectedly retarded by frequent swells of water in the Miami, overflowing the land, and removing the fence, after it was made, from its proper place. They, however, by continued exertions, prepared a large field for planting, which might probably have been planted in time had the Indians not stolen their horses when they left to return home to attend to their summer crop. The last named loss and the want of a sufficient quantity of seed corn were severely felt; so that it was too late before the corn was in the ground for it to ripen. During the summer, health and uninterrupted peace with the Indians prevailed, and the new settlements were continually increasing in numerical strength, but they labored under great difficulties in tending their corn for the want of teams, plows, etc., but autumn brought with it its difficulties. In September, some of the hunters reported signs of Indians, and as they did not come in to trade as they did in the previous winter, it was feared their designs were hostile; but soon all doubt was removed. Towards the close of September Mr. Soward sent two of his sons (John and Ziba) to the corn-field for some green corn, who on their way out were surrounded by a party of Indians, as was afterwards learned from Ziba. Not returning, the inhabitants of the fort became very uneasy, and preparation was made to go in search of them early in the morning, should they not return by that time. As soon as it was light, all the men that could be spared from the fort, went in pursuit of the missing boys, dividing into small parties. Messrs. Luke Foster and John

Clawson took the direct path that was usually traveled to the corn-field, within a short distance of which, in crossing a large tree that had fallen across the path, they found Ziba on his elbows and knees, with his forehead nearly imbedded in the earth, and his scalp, including all the skin with hair on it, stripped off, and the marks of three strokes of the tomahawk on one side of his head, each of which had perforated the skull and passed into the brain, who, though apparently insensible, was still living. Mr. Clawson, who was a remarkably large and strong man, proposed to Mr. Foster that if he would assist in getting him on his shoulders he would take him to the fort, which he did, carrying him in that way more than three-fourths of a mile. No physician could be had to dress his wound, but all that could be done with the skill they possessed was done to soothe his pains. After washing and dressing his wounds, he for a time revived, and told his friends that as he and his brother were going to the corn-field they were suddenly surrounded by a party of Indians; that they felt very much alarmed; that one of the Indians said to them in English: "Do not be frightened; you are safe;" that he then took a halter from his bosom and commenced to tie John, on seeing which, he started to run for home, and was followed by some Indians, but kept ahead of them until he came to the tree across the road, when he was knocked down, and knew nothing more. He lingered in his sufferings for a number of days and died. Three days after this distressing occurrence a Mr. Larkin, as he was returning from the woods, found the head of John stuck on the top of a hickory pole, which had been bent over, the top cut off and sharpened, and his body on the ground. This circumstance ended all friendly intercourse with the Indians until Wayne's treaty in 1795. Notwithstanding the dark shade this event cast over their prospects, there was no choice left them but to persevere in their efforts—retreat was impossible—danger must be met at every point; it was with them truly a critical period.   They, however, breasted the storm, and, after years of toil, war and bloodshed, succeeded in effecting what they had undertaken.

Yours truly,   E. F.

Published Jan. 24, 1851.

———

LETTER VII.

MR. TORBET—Unlike farmers in old settled countries, after the corn crop was laid by, our new settlers had no labor to perform to occupy their time profitably to themselves.   To remedy that evil Major Stites had nearly all the bottom lands at Columbia laid off in five-acre lots from the fort down to the plat of that part he laid off in half-acre for a town, and from the river back to Turkey Bottom, which he offered for sale on reasonable terms, giving every man an opportunity to become a land-owner, and, to such as did not wish to buy, he gave leases for three years on condition they would clear and fence the lots they leased.   Many embraced the opportunity to buy or lease, and went to work to prepare for a crop the next season.   Unfortunately, the crop then growing did not ripen before frost, so that it was scarcely fit for bread and totally unfit for planting.   In anticipation of the difficulties that might result from that state of things, Mr. Hezekiah Stites, accompanied by two other men who wished to return to the old settlements, was dispatched on a trip to the Red Stone country for a supply of breadstuff and seed-corn, and did ascend the Ohio and Monongahela to that place, in a canoe, which they propelled with poles and paddles against the stream, undisturbed by the Indians, and returned the ensuing spring with his supply.   In the meantime the tide of emigration was so great that the supply brought on by Mr.

Stites was entirely insufficient, and many of the settlers were driven to the necessity of going through the woods to Lexington, Ky., for seed-corn. In the early part of December seven persons, viz., Isaac Ferris, John Ferris, Jonah Reynolds, William Goforth, John S. Gano, Daniel Bates and Luther Kitchel arrived about the same time with their families; the two latter passed on to Cincinnati. With these families there were several men without families, viz., Benjamin Alcut, Libeus Marshal, Abraham Ferris and others; add to these, families almost daily arriving, and the fort would soon fill to overflowing, many of the small apartments being occupied by two and three families at one time. It was rather fortunate at that time that they were not cumbered with much furniture. For chairs, they used three-legged stools; for tables, chests or large boxes; and their beds at night were spread on the rough floor. I do not remember of but one chair in the fort. Forced by necessity, several cabins were built outside the fort. Major Goforth built a two-story hewed log-house, which was as well prepared for defense as the fort was. Among the outsiders I recollect Captain Davis, Mr. Newel, Mr. Mills and Mr. Isaac Ferris. About the close of December Mr. David Jones, a minister of the Baptist Church in Pennsylvania, who had been a chaplain in the Revolutionary under General Wayne, arrived at Cincinnati, in company with the reinforcement of soldiers (I believe under Major Daugherty), in the character of a chaplain, but finding no encouragement to preach there he came to Ft. Miami; he preached the first sermons ever preached in the new settlements. The sermon was preached in the block-house in the southwest corner of the fort—the congregation was large, but had to stand on their feet for want of seats. I was too young to comprehend and judge of the merits of the discourse, but recollect it was full of encouragement; the people were exhorted to put their confidence for defense in the arm of an Omnipotent God, and he would drive

out their enemies before them and give them as an inheritance
the goodly land.   Mr. Jones, not liking the service, soon returned to Pennsylvania.   This brings me to the close of 1789,
a little more than thirteen months from the time the first five
families landed to take possession of the country.

Yours truly,   E. F.

Lawrenceburg, Ind., Jan. 26, 1851.

LETTER VIII.

Mr. Torbet—In sketching in former numbers my recollections of the early settlements of the Miami country I wrote
mostly what has been communicated to me from others, of
what they had heard and seen, hereafter I shall write mostly
what I have myself heard and seen.   The early settlers in the
commencement of 1790 felt an increased confidence in their
ability to repel any general attack the Indians might make
upon them.   The increase of numerical strength at Columbia, Cincinnati and North Bend—the settlement of Dunlap's
station on the Big Miami, and Covalt's station on the Little
Miami, left but little ground to fear that any serious attack
would be made on the older stations.   The winter was ex-
ceedingly pleasant, during the whole of which there was no
snow, nor but very little frost, so that for a time there appeared to be no difficulty thrown in the way to hinder the
most persevering industry in preparing the largest possible
amount of land for cultivation for the ensuing season, but
while dreaming of prosperity a dark cloud suddenly passed
over.   Mr. Abel Cook, one of the first party who had landed
at Columbia to commence the new settlement there, while attempting to travel from Covalt's station, was waylaid and
killed by the Indians.   News of that sad event soon reached

the fort, and a sufficient number of volunteers immediately
started in search of his body, which was found a short distance from the path that had been marked out to guide the
traveler in going to the station, and near where Armstrong's
upper mills were afterwards built. The body of Mr. Cook
was brought in and interred, but it was not known to what
tribe the aggressors belonged, or how many there were in the
party.   It was supposed by the militia who went out to bring
the body in that he was at first slightly wounded, and attempted to escape by flight, but was pursued and overtaken;
that he made a desperate defense from the appearance of the
ground around where the body lay, but was overcome by
superior numbers, killed and scalped.   This melancholy event
taught them that whatever security they might have against
a general attack, there was no safety for them when scattered
in the woods.   In the month of March the attention of the
people was turned away from their corn-field to their sugar
crops, for until that month the weather had not been cold
enough for making sugar.   Not long after the excitement
occasioned by the above related circumstance was allayed
another cry of Indian alarm called the people from their slum-
ber; I recollect being awakened from my sleep by the noise
and confusion, and that the first sound in my ears that I could
understand was, ''Turn out for the Indians are coming!''
There was one universal rush among the militia from their
cabins to the open space inside the fort.   A messenger from
Cincinnati had arrived bringing the intelligence that Dunlap's
station was besieged by the Indians, that a Mr. Abner Hunt
had been taken by the Indians the evening before, and that
after an unsuccessful attempt to use him as an instrument to
prevail on Lieutenant Kingsbury to surrender they had killed
him and made a general attack, and that a Mr. John W.
Wallace (I believe it was) offered his service to creep through
the Indians, under cover of the darkness of the night, and

make his way to the new settlements for assistance. He first arrived at Cincinnati, but it was thought there could not be a sufficient force raised there, not being able to judge the number of Indians engaged in the attack, and therefore he was sent to Columbia for further assistance. The first suggestion made was that it might be a feint, on the part of the Indians, to attack that place with a small party, to draw away the militia from the stronger points, where they could strike a more fatal blow, but there was no time for delay. In a short time the whole body of the militia, except a few of the most aged, who were left to protect the fort, were on their march for Dunlap's station. In about twenty hours they returned and reported that on their approach to the station the Indians fled, but on ascertaining the course of their trail it was feared they intended an attack either on Columbia or Covalt's station. A messenger was sent to the latter place to warn them of their supposed danger, and the night was spent in the fort to put it in a better condition for defense. The men reported that the people at the station had made a most gallant defense, and that the women had proved themselves heroines, that they not only personally visited the men at their posts, and furnished them with food and drink, but encouraged them to acquit themselves like men, and when their lead was like to fail melted their pewter spoons and plates and run them into balls. During the balance of the war the valor of the Colerain heroines was oft referred to as worthy of imitation, and as one of the means by which the inhabitants of that place were preserved from indiscriminate slaughter.   Yours truly,   E. F.

Published Feb. 7, 1851.

LETTER IX.

MR. TORBET—In my last I made an allusion to the encouraging prospects the early settlers had when they entered upon the labors of 1790; but purposely omitted to speak of the productiveness of soil as one source of encouragement. The agriculturist whose principal hope (for the time being) depends on a good crop of corn can not be otherwise than pleased with a fertile soil, which, if properly cultivated, and Providence should send sufficient rain, gives full assurance of an ample reward for his labor. The soil at Columbia, though it had not been fairly tried with those domestic vegetables which constitute the usual variety wanted for the comfort and support of civilized men, was so rich and mellow, and had, without the aid of cultivation, produced such rich pastures and beautiful forests, that none could doubt that when subdued and brought into cultivation, it would more than amply reward all the labor bestowed upon it. By the dint of labor, they had cleared, fenced and prepared as much land of that character for cultivation as they, with the strength they then had, could work to good advantage, so that when the season should roll around, they had in prospect a full supply of bread as a stimulus to persevering industry. I have no doubt but many of the present citizens of Columbia and the surrounding country would feel an interest in reading a correct reply to an inquiry often made by strangers, when they happen to fall in company with any of the surviving pioneers of the Miami valley : "What was the appearance of the country at that time?" For the gratification of such, should this letter meet their eye, I will answer—romantic. It was then the temporary residence of the red wild man at certain seasons of the year, and at all times the range of the bear, the deer, the wildcat, the raccoon, the opossum and wild turkey, with numerous other animals ranging on the green pastures at all seasons, and during most of the fall and winter months glutting themselves with the rich fruits of the forests. On approaching the shore at the mouth of the Little Miami, you would see the banks of both rivers beautifully lined with rows of cotton-wood and water maple. Rising to the first level there was a mixture of the honey-locust, hackberry and box-elder, interspersed with very large sycamores, the latter most generally near the rivers. Rising to a still higher level you would enter an extensive plain covered over with as rich a growth of forest trees as the eye of man could wish to look upon. There was the oak, the ash, the walnut, the hickory, the beech, the sugar tree and the buckeye, all growing together, and towering toward the skies, as though they had been vieing with each other for ages which should rise highest in the air, so as to catch the first rays of the morning sun, or which should spread its boughs to the widest extent so as to form the coolest retreat for the weary traveler seeking a shelter from the scorching heat of the noon-day summer sun. Among the rest there was one sycamore that might with some propriety be called the king of the forest. This tree stood a few rods back from the bank of the Ohio river, about eighty rods below Fort Miami. Of its height I can not speak; but it must have far out-topped the most lofty of the other trees, for after resisting the pressure of the stormy winds (probably for centuries) it had been forced at last to yield to some furious tornado that had passed over the land; which separated the top and part of the trunk from the main portion of the body at (as I should judge) about the height of eighty feet, where I think it was still about six feet in diameter. The body of this sycamore was sixteen feet six inches in diameter near the ground and had a hollow of fifteen which continued in a proportionate size to where the top was broken off. It diminished in size as it ascended very gradually, and was remarkably straight, and had very smooth outside bark for so large a tree. On the northwest side of the tree there was an opening large enough for a man on horseback to enter. I knew a gentleman once to ride into the tree, with a lady on behind him, who turned around and came out again without any difficulty. It became a place of resort to the inhabitants of the fort, who, when they wanted to take a pleasant walk, and were not deterred by fear of Indians, more frequently visited this large tree than any other place. The description here given is taken from my own personal view and recollection of it, and in no way exaggerated. I suppose I have seen it more than a thousand times. But lofty, aged and strong as it was, when deprived of the protection it received from smaller surrounding trees, it was forced to yield to the pressure of an immense mass of drift which floated and lodged against it in the extraordinary flood of 1793, and accumulated until by the force of the current it was broken off at the bend of the ground and forced into the Ohio, from whence it descended to parts unknown. This beautiful plain was covered in many places with an undergrowth, mostly of spice bark and papaw, and everywhere with a coat of wild grass and other vegetables which at all seasons of the year afforded a full bite pasture for all the cattle owned by the citizens until subdued and brought under cultivation, but could not be used for their horses without exposing them to be stolen and taken away by the Indians. Yours with respect, E. F.

Published Feb. 14, 1851.

———

LETTER X.

MR. TORBET—Many other circumstances, other than those heretofore named, operated on the fears and hopes of the early settler. Many of them had been raised in opulence,

18

and had indulged in many of the luxuries and enjoyed all the necessaries of life; now removed far from their former homes, where nothing but the most common fare could be had, and that often in stinted measure, were cast down, "though not forsaken." I recollect hearing it said, and suppose it is true, that Mrs. Rhoda Stites (a mother who had three children) was one day so deeply affected with the danger of starvation, if they should escape the barbarity of the Indians, that she started to seek a place of retirement in the woods where she might alone give vent to her grief. While pursuing a narrow track a short distance from the fort, she approached within a few steps of an Indian before she discovered him, and was so affrighted that she turned around, as she was permitted to do undisturbed by the Indian (who, she supposed, saw her cheeks bedewed with tears), and made her way back to the fort, rejoicing that she had escaped the danger to which she had just been exposed. Add to the want of bread the mortification of an American mother, who had been in the habit at all times of clothing her children comfortably, and sometimes ornamenting them to please her own fancy, must feel to see them clad in rags and dirt, for the want of materials to make new ones of, or soap to wash them when dirty, and you will see enough to discourage and depress them. As yet there was no shoemaker, tailor, blacksmith, weaver, or any other mechanic's shop; nor was there a mill in the country to grind their grain, should they chance to procure any, save such as were turned by hand. But admit all these difficulties, they indulged a hope that better times awaited them. In the early part of this year they were visited by Elder John Mason, Baptist preacher from Kentucky, and the Rev. Mr. Rice, a Presbyterian from the same state, both of whom preached to the people in the fort. They were likewise encouraged with the prospect of a school for the education of their children. Mr. Frey, a young gentleman from

Freysburg, N. H., opened a school in one of the block-houses in the fort, which, when built, was designated for that purpose. This was the first school ever taught in the Miami country. Early in this year Governor Arthur St. Clair arrived in the Miami country accompanied with some judges, vested with authority from congress to establish a civil government in the northwestern territory. At Columbia he appointed Major William Goforth a justice of the peace, and Mr. Joseph Gerrard, constable, with instructions (if my recollection is correct) to perform the several functions of their offices in conformity with the laws of Pennsylvania until further provisions should be made. The governor also appointed Mr. James Flinn captain, Mr. John Ferris, lieutenant, and Mr. Elijah Stites engineer of a militia company at Columbia, with authority to enroll, discipline and call into service the militia when circumstances might require it; but what was more pleasing than all, they were now promised an army, which should come shortly with sufficient strength to chastise and drive back the Indians. The advance of this promised army, shortly after, arrived under command of General Harmar, which was hailed with enthusiastic joy, and greatly strengthened their confidence. All these circumstances taken together instilled fresh vigor into their minds, and with the means they had they went to work and raised a bountiful crop; which, but for the increase of emigration, would have more than supplied their want of corn. Another circumstance full of encouragement—a Mr. Coleman, who was an extraordinary genius for a man of his information, undertook, and actually built, a mill in a flat-bottom boat capable of grinding their corn. This boat was placed below a fish dam made by the citizens across the Little Miami about half a mile above its mouth, and fastened to the shore by a rope, so that when they wanted it to grind it was shoved out so that the water pitching over the fish pit in the dam would fall on the water-wheel and start the mill to grinding, and when they wanted it to stop they drew it to shore where the water was turned away from the wheel. This mill worked well for a time, but unfortunately in the fall of the year, and when most wanted, a flood in the Miami swept it out into the Ohio river and they saw it no more, and the citizens had again to turn to their hand mills. Harmar's campaign was, however, the all engrossing topic for the time. By it they expected to be delivered from all further danger of Indians, and permitted to pursue their labor in perfect peace.

The march, progress and termination of the campaign shall be the subject of my next letter.

Yours truly,   E. F.
Lawrenceburg, Feb. 18, 1851.

LETTER XI.

MR. TORBET—In the following communication, I do not pretend to write from information received officially. There was at that time no newspaper in the country through which official communications could be made to reach the people; consequently they had to depend upon public rumor, and by it they formed their opinion of men and things, and, whether true or false, if believed, it had the same effect upon their hopes and fears. They knew it was a fact, that early in the year 1790, General Josiah Harmar arrived among them with a number of soldiers, which, rumor said, was but the advance of an army shortly to arrive, sufficient in number to drive the Indians back, and to compel them to ask for peace, and consent to a favorable treaty. Though General Harmar established his headquarters at Cincinnati, as it was then said, in accordance with the wishes of Judge Symmes and Major Stites, as being the most central place from which all the different stations could get help if attacked by the Indians, he often visited Columbia, it still being the most populous station among the new settlements—and by his appearance and the encouragement he gave for a prosperous campaign greatly strengthened their hopes; so that there was but one opinion about his final success. The expected result created great anxiety for the speedy accomplishment of what they so much desired, and every week's delay was a source of uneasiness. It was, however, understood that the general was authorized to raise one thousand mounted volunteer militia from Kentucky, and that he expected additional forces (and military supplies) down the river, the arrival of whom must necessarily occasion considerable delay; but still there was such an intense anxiety to see him march, that many complaints were uttered about his tardy movements. At length, after spring and summer had been spent in preparation, about the last of September the general took up his line of march with an army of about fifteen hundred men under his command, to the inexpressible joy of all citizens, and almost certain expectation of a triumphant victory. In the military forces of the Kentucky mounted men, they had unbounded confidence, and in the interview they had with General Harmar they had formed a very favorable opinion of him, and now their impatience was raised to hear the result. On leaving Ft. Washington the army marched up Deer creek to the first fork, then ascended the point of the hill near to the place where the Walnut Hill road leaves the Reading turnpike, and over the country between the waters of Mill creek and Duck creek, crossing Sycamore and Turtle creek in a direction east of north until they came to the waters of the Little Miami, near Deerfield, opening as they passed along a track for the army, afterward known by the early settlers as "Harmar's trace," which became the principal thoroughfare many years, for white men and Indians in passing out and in, from and to the river. After coming to the waters of the Little Miami, they passed up on the west side of the river near to the mouth of Sugar creek, where they crossed over to the east side of the river, and kept up the valley, several days' march, to an Indian village, called Old Chillicothe, where they changed their course, recrossed the river, and took a northwesterly direction, crossed Mad river, and the Big Miami on a direct course to the Miami villages on the St. Joseph, near to where the town of Ft. Wayne now stands. There they came to a halt, and, after a few partial engagements with the enemy, retraced their steps and returned to Ft. Washington early in November, being absent one month and five days. The news that the army had returned without any general engagement with the enemy produced one general burst of indignation. It was said that on several occasions a minority of the army had met the Indians, and in an unequal contest had been able to hold them in check until exhausted, when they were compelled to withdraw, leaving the enemy so crippled that they dare not presume to follow, while the main body of the army were retained in camp, and had no share in the engagement, and that while the officers who had been exposed to all the dangers of the contest were imploring further assistance, with the assurance of victory, if they could obtain but a small reinforcement, the general issued a general order to take up the line of march and return to Ft. Washington. All their reports, whether true or not, had their influence on the public minds, and excited the most intent opposition to the commanding general. The militia threw all the blame on the commander, while the officers of the regular army threw it all back on the insurbordination of the militia. The people believed the former, and seemed for a time prepared to make a sacrifice of him to appease their vengeance. The bearing of so unexpected a retreat (after an absence of only about five weeks), with the loss of about two hundred men, upon the future prospect of the country, it was thought would be very unfavorable. It is true it was afterward reported that the Indians lost as many as the white people, but that is all conjecture on our side, while the Indians knew, almost to a man, what our loss was. It was also said they had destroyed the growing crop and towns of the Indians ; but while some viewed that as favorable, others thought it would only exasperate them, and excite to a more cruel, barbarous and destructive warfare on their side.

The whole campaign was considered a failure, and it was thought the whole country was now exposed to invasions and continued depredations from an enemy so exasperated ; that he would struggle hard for revenge. The question was, what shall be done? To retreat was impossible; to collect the militia and place them in a situation to defend against the enemy would be to jeopardize every interest of the country, except personal safety ; and even that in the end would be lost by a state of starvation; the largest proportion of their corn being in Turkey Bottom, about a mile from the fort, and could not be gathered and brought in without being continually exposed to danger. While all these difficulties were staring them in the face, it seemed to be a source of consolation to many that, if they could do nothing more, they could at least, with their tongues, wreak their vengeance on the head of their unfortunate general. After a short time's consideration, it was found that the militia in Columbia had increased to one hundred and fifty, in Cincinnati to one hundred, at North Bend to eighty, Dunlap's Station to fifteen, and Covalt's Station to twenty. Two new companies were formed at Columbia, and Mr. John S. Gano was appointed captain of one, with Mr. Ephraim Kibbey, lieutenant, and a Mr. Hall, captain of the other, and they were ordered to muster their companies every week   Orders were also given to see that every person enrolled as a militiaman should carry his gun and be equipped ready for fight, at all gatherings, whether on the Sabbath or other days. Thus it will be seen that a dark cloud hung over the new settlements for a time, and eclipsed all the pleasing anticipations indulged in at the commencement of the year. Yours truly, E. F. *Lawrenceburg, Feb. 22, 1891.*

LETTER XII.

MR. TORBET—In my last letter, in order to carry my recollection of the influence of Harmar's campaign on the minds of the people and its bearing on the prosperity of the settlements to its termination, I passed over other circumstances, worthy of a passing notice. The expected success of Harmar in driving the Indians back brought an increased number of emigrants to the country, among them the families of Broadwell, Buckingham, Light, Morris, Biddle, Clark, Crosly and others, whose descendants are still residing in the country, to witness the results of the enterprise and industry of their fathers. The school heretofore spoken of was soon broken up on account of a difficulty between Mr. Frey and his landlord. He was, however, soon succeeded by a Mr. Ayreheart, who continued the school for one quarter; then gave way to a Mr. Thomas Haman, an accomplished teacher and gentleman (from Ireland), who continued the school nine months longer to the satisfaction of all. I will here mention as a part of history that some may feel an interest in that in the month of March, 1790, Elder Stephen Gano, a Baptist preacher, then from the city of New York, who had come to the west to visit an aged father in Kentucky, came also to Columbia to visit a brother (the late John S. Gano), and there found nine persons who had been members of Baptist churches in the parts from which they came, and who wished to be organized into a church. He organized them as such, and on the ensuing Sabbath added to them three others, by administering to them for the church the ordinance of baptism. This was the first organized religious church in the Miami country, and still exists, and is known by the name of the "Duck Creek Church." The increase of emigration was so great this season that many families ventured to build cabins and remove down to the town, about one mile below the fort, and so great was the increase that before the close of the year the town outnumbered the fort in population. There was also another settlement made this year on the east side of the Miami, called Gerrard station, consisting probably of from ten to fifteen families. The season this year was very favorable for a crop, and the yield an abundant one, for the amount of land cultivated, and what was very extraordinary—in almost all their fields, but more abundantly in the lower lands near the Miami river, there was a plentiful crop of squashes, without planting, consisting of various species, not less that ten to fifteen, which were found to be very useful. These were preserved as a substitute for potatoes, and thought by many to be fully equal to them. There was also an extensive crop of excellent pumpkins, which, had they had flour for crust, and shortening, spice and milk, would have enabled them to indulge in the free use of pumpkin pies; but for the want of other materials they could only be used for pumpkin bread by mixing it with corn meal and baking it. The Indians were less troublesome this year than the several succeeding ones. I do not remember any other injury done by them, after the commencement of spring, than stealing a few horses about planting time. I believe there was one Indian scalp taken that year by a white man while out hunting. Taking the result of Harmar's campaign into view, in connection with all the circumstances that operated on the hopes

and fears of the people, the same dark cloud that hung over
their prospects in the commencement of the season still dark-
ened their horizon, and they had to enter upon a new year in
the same state of suspense they had entered the last one, ex-
cepting an increasing confidence (growing out of their numerical strength) that they would be able to resist any attack
the Indians might make upon them.

Very truly,   E. F.

Lawrenceburg, March 7, 1851.

LETTER XIII.

MR. TORBET—The most gloomy apprehensions entertained
by the people in the new settlements, about the results of Harmar's campaign, in 1790, were realized to the fullest extent
in 1791. Emboldened by Harmar's precipitate retreat from
the Miami town on the St. Joseph, back to Fort Washington, and the small loss of life the Indians reported that they
had sustained in their successful resistance to his attack, they
began early in the season to hover round the frontier settlements, and in the end there was more bloodshed and slaughter that year than any other during the seven years' war.
Very early in the year they commenced their depredations by
stealing all the horses they could possibly get hold of, and in
this they were so bold that one night, the gates of the fort
being left open through carelessness, they entered the fort and
stole two horses that had been taken inside and tied by halters
for safety. Early in the spring a Mr. Dimett, in company
with Mr. Jonathan Coleman, in traveling from Columbia to
Covalt's Station, were waylaid by a party of Indians, who
killed and scalped the former, and, it was supposed, carried
the other away a captive, as no trace of his body was found.

I believe he was never heard of afterwards by his friends. The Indians not only harassed the frontier settlements, but they collected in large numbers about the mouth of the Scioto river, as was supposed, if possible, to prevent emigration to the country. The first certain evidence had of their strength by the white people was in the slaughter of Colonel Strong's party of soldiers, the remnant of Harmar's army, whose term, of service had expired. Colonel Strong had been ordered to march them to Fort Harmar, near Marietta, and discharge them; so it was reported. On their way up the river from Fort Washington they stopped the first night at Columbia, where, as far as they could, they exchanged the flour they had drawn for corn bread—by which many who had not tasted wheat bread for many a day had an opportunity of having warm biscuit for breakfast. I very well recollect how I relished the rare treat. Colonel Strong had a keel-boat in which the provisions and camp equipage was transported, which was rowed up stream by a number of soldiers. There was a cabin in the boat fixed up for the officers in which, it was said, they rode, and the men traveled up the shore on foot, using the boat for a ferry in crossing the mouth of the streams of water in their way. I do not know that it was reported how many men there were, but should suppose, from my recollection of their appearance, there were not less than two or three hundred. A few days after passing Columbia, up stream, the keel-boat, with a few of the men, returned on their way back to Fort Washington, and landed again at Columbia and made the following report: On their way up they passed undisturbed until they approached the mouth of the Scioto, where the boat landed to ferry the men across, and when they were stepping into the boat a large body of Indians rushed suddenly from ambush and formed a line in their rear, and, with tomahawks and knives, making the most hideous yells, they rushed furiously on them, and commenced the work of slaughter. The soldiers made no resistance. Being instantly cut off from a retreat to the woods they tried to crowd into the boat until it was like to sink, and was, by order of the commandant, shoved off, leaving the most men on shore to the mercy of the savages—many of whom plunged into the river to swim for the boat, and were drowned, and those left on shore were indiscriminately slain. The Indians, or a part of them, followed the boat for some distance, keeping up a fire from their rifles; but she was soon rowed out of their reach, not, however, without receiving the impression of a great many balls shot into her sides. I believe there were some men killed and wounded in the boat. This was the most distressing slaughter of white people that had as yet been made and created great alarm.

A few days after the return of Colonel Strong, a flat-boat hove in view—the first that had made its appearance since the colonel's return. The boat was discovered by some of the school boys just as they were dismissed for dinner; I recollect hearing one of the school boys cry out, "Yonder comes a flat-boat," to which another responded, "She must have run the gauntlet to get here; let us go and see," at which word we all ran down to the river where the boat was landing. I was in the crowd, and so was Judge Isaac Dunn, who, with myself, is a living witness of the shattered and bloody appearance of the boat. On landing it was ascertained that the boat was owned by Mr. William Plasket, who had his family on board, and who made the following report: that he was descending the river in company with two other families by the name of Greathouse, each of whom occupied separate boats, and that in each boat there were several passengers, not belonging to the families, who were descending the river to see the country. At the time they drew near to the Scioto river the other two boats were something like half a mile in advance of his, and that, on looking out, he saw several canoes loaded with Indians go out and take possession of both boats without resistance, and that both of them were immediately landed. For him to retreat was impossible. If he attempted to land he could not make the shore much short of the spot where the Indians were, and as they were supplied with canoes, they could attack him on either side; so that in his mind the only question was, shall we fight or die? He chose the former and prepared for action. The first thing was to examine the guns on board, nine in number, and see that they were all loaded. He then, with an ax, split off the top of the board, next to the roof of the boat, so as to make room to shoot through if attacked. He then directed his son William to lie down in the bottom of the boat and load the guns after they were discharged, soon as handed to him. He next placed the men in a row in a position to fire, but not until he gave orders, and directed his wife and children to lie down on the bottom of the boat, and not to stir or make any noise on any consideration. As they came opposite the mouth of the river, three canoes, with three Indians in each, approached them from the shore, when Mr. Plasket directed them each to shoot so that no two should point at the same Indian, and to await his order before they fired. He permitted them to come so near that he supposed they had concluded he would make no resistance, and dropped their paddles and reached out their hands to take hold of the boat, when, at the word "fire," each shot, and killed six of the Indians; the other three tacked about and made for the shore, at which time as many (they supposed) as five hundred Indians appeared on the shore and commenced firing on them; but by exertions they soon passed some small stream below, and the Indians gave up the chase. In the struggle they had two killed and two wounded, and lost all the horses and cows they had. Before arriving at Columbia they had landed and buried the dead and threw their dead horses and cows overboard.

These melancholy events made the impression at first that immigration must be so interrupted as to prevent the arrival of any more families. But in this they were disappointed, for the Indians soon left the rivers and returned to their town; after, as was supposed, having massacred the two families they had taken. They were never heard of by the settlers in the new country. Yours truly,   E. F.
March 14, 1851.

LETTER XIV.

The circumstances related in my last letter were of such a discouraging character that the most gloomy apprehensions were still pressing on the minds of the people, and left no other hope than that they would be able to defend themselves, which hope was strengthened by the continual influx of population. Among the arrivals which were daily taking place at all the stations along the river were John Smith and family, John Ludlow and family, Colonel Oliver Spencer and family, Francis Dunlevy, John Riley, and many others who were afterwards known as taking an active part in the public affairs of the new country. I recollect one arrival of nine families, viz.: David, Joseph, Daniel, Jacob and Stephen Reeder, who were brothers; Thomas Hubbell, who was a brother-in-law, and William Harper, Jeremiah Brann and Mr. Tingley, who had married daughters of the Reeders. To strengthen the hope growing out of the tide of emigration continually setting in, it was rumored that an expedition was preparing in Kentucky to march to the Indian towns and attack them in their own villages, and teach them the necessity of staying at home to protect their wives and children and fire-sides, and, by that means, draw them off from our frontiers. The rumor proved true, and, in the month of May, General Charles

Scott crossed the Ohio river at the mouth of the Kentucky, with eight hundred mounted men, and moved forward with such rapidity that he reached and attacked several of the Indian towns on the Wabash before they had notice of his approach. In this expedition General Scott killed a number of warriors, took fifty-four prisoners, destroyed a large amount of property, and returned in triumph with very little loss. The news of this brilliant affair, as it spread, infused joy and gladness into the minds of the people. It was soon rumored that the success attending this expedition had influenced General St. Clair to start a second one, under the command of General Wilkinson, which was confirmed early in August, by his arrival at Ft. Washington with five hundred mounted Kentucky riflemen. From thence he moved forward to the Indian towns on Eel river, near its mouth—took several of their villages by surprise, killed a number of warriors, captured thirty-four prisoners and returned with but very trifling loss—increasing the joy of the people to something like enthusiasm. Now, the people said, "The scale of war has turned, victory perches on our brow, and we hope soon to have peace." The prisoners taken by Scott and Wilkinson were brought to Cincinnati, where they were treated with all the kindness that circumstances would admit; but at what time, or how liberated, I do not recollect. It was next rumored that if the success of the two expeditions named failed to bring the Indians to terms, another grand expedition, under the command of General St. Clair, in person, would march into the heart of the Indian country, take possession of some of their principal towns, fortify themselves and continue a military force among them. This campaign and its results shall be the subject of my next letter.

Yours truly,   E. F.

Lawrenceburg, March 17, 1851.

LETTER XV.

MR. TORBET—In my recollection of the march, progress and final result of General St. Clair's campaign in 1791, I wish it to be understood that I do not intend to impute to any one the cause of the misfortunes attending that enterprise. That the general was a patriot I have no doubt; and that he was a man of superior mind and acquirements has been so well established that it need not be re-asserted; of his military skill I am not capable of judging, but know he was unfortunate. In the commencement of his campaign, following so soon after the brilliant victories of Scott and Wilkinson (which were said to have been projected by him), the people had an unshaken confidence in his prospects of success. No application for a treaty having been made by the Indians, early in September the army took up the line of march for the Indian towns, and on their way erected a fort on the east bank of the Big Miami, called Fort Hamilton, where the town of Hamilton is now located. After having finished that fort they again moved forward, and at the distance of about forty miles erected another fort, called Fort Jefferson. The site of this fort is within the present bounds of Darke county, and about six miles from the county seat. After having erected the last-named fort, they again continued their march for the Indian towns. Information of their progress had been heard by expresses arriving almost daily, and this was generally of an encouraging character; but after leaving Fort Jefferson it was reported that the terms of service of the men were daily expiring, and that they were demanding their discharges, and returning, so that the army was continually diminishing; and that provisions were short and that the men were put on half rations. Desertions and insubordinations were also spoken of, and, on the whole, the prospect was less encouraging than it had been; still, as to the final result, but little doubt was expressed. The Indians were to be humbled and compelled to sue for peace.

Thus matters connected with the movements of the army stood in the minds of the people at Columbia on the morning of the 8th of November. What was the feeling at Cincinnati, or the other stations, I know not, but so it was with us; yet final success was not seriously doubted.

On the morning of that melancholy day, as it proved to be, I was employed, by the direction of my father, in filling corn baskets with corn, on the outside of the fort, for a neighbor who had a husking the evening before, and was putting away his corn for safekeeping in an upper room, or, as they term it, the loft. While thus engaged a man appeared, coming from the woods, ragged and dirty, and, as he said, nearly starving with hunger, who reported that he had escaped the destruction of St. Clair's army. His story was, that on the morning of the 4th they were attacked by an overwhelming force of Indians, and that after three hours hard fighting, during which time the most of St. Clair's men were slain, the Indians rushed upon them, and that the whole army had been slain—that, so far as he knew, he was the only man that had escaped. He also said that he had eaten nothing since his escape but some haws he picked up under a haw tree he passed in the woods on his way, and a part of a dead turkey he had found in the woods on his way, without being cooked. The report brought by this man, passed with almost the rapidity of lightning through the fort; but its effects were in part stayed by the opinion of some woodsmen (or, as they were often called at that time, Indian hunters), that the man was a deserter, and had made up this tale to prevent being taken up as such; he, however, continued to affirm that what he had said was true. While questioning, and partly insult-

19

ing the man, another appeared, telling the same tale, except that more than the first man had supposed had escaped the general slaughter; this last man was almost instantly followed by two others, who confirmed the same facts. Imagination can not describe the scene that ensued. Very few families were there who had not friends in the campaign, bearing the relation of husband, father, brother, or child. There was, indeed, weeping and wailing, and a refusal to be comforted. I had a brother with them, and, perhaps, my melancholy feelings were increased by the grief and wailings of a mother on his account. To me the heavens appeared to be shrouded in sable, and though the sun was shining the atmosphere around appeared like the "troubled waters"; all around was dark and gloomy. The state of suspense, however, hanging over the mind in relation to friends was gradually removed, and before bedtime that evening, so far as I can recollect, all that went from Columbia, except two (James Bailey and Isaac Morris, who were killed), had returned or were heard from. Captain Gano (as he was then termed) had a severe wound from a ball passing through one arm, but returned, in other respects, safe. He, it was said, manifested the bravery of a true soldier during the battle, and covered himself with glory. This, of all others, was, at Columbia, the most gloomy and trying time the inhabitants of the new country had passed through, and presented the most dark and gloomy prospect of any event that had yet occurred. Some thought, as they said, further resistance would be vain; that the Indians would be in on us in such numbers that we should be compelled to fly before them; but others thought best to strengthen the fort, and hold on to it as a place of retreat, if assailed, and that we should still be able to repel any invasion. But all agreed that the campaign was an entire failure, and that the people had nothing now to depend upon but their own personal and private resources. The unfortunate general, who had a few weeks before marched out at the head of more than three thousand men, full of expectation, and had now returned with less than six hundred, having lost the balance by discharge, desertion and death in the field of battle, nearly (it was said) a thousand in the latter, while it was supposed the Indians did not lose more than about sixty, was now the object of their most bitter denunciations. This campaign, carried on at a very great expense, and attended with so great a loss of human life, was considered the most unfortunate attempt yet made to bring the enemy to terms; but I have already spun my letter to too great a length, and must therefore close.   Yours truly,   E. F.

Lawrenceburg, March 20, 1851.

LETTER XVI.

MR. TORBET—The most gloomy apprehensions among the people, about the result of St. Clair's defeat, were in a great measure realized. Marauding parties of Indians were soon hovering around all our settlements, stealing horses and killing our men, if they ventured from home, or capturing and carrying them off as prisoners. To prevent these disastrous consequences, block-houses were erected on the hills, beyond the outside limits of the settlement at Columbia, and the militia were called out in small parties to keep up a line of communication from one to the other, and, if possible, prevent Indians from entering the settlement and attacking the people without being first discovered; but all, apparently, to no purpose, for the Indians would still pass their lines undiscovered, commit depredations and escape unpunished. Notwithstanding all these discouraging circumstances, there were others of a cheering character. Among them, not the least important, a Mr. Wickerham had built a tub-mill east of the Little Miami, near the mouth of Clough creek, which was capable of grinding a large amount of corn; thereby, relieving them from the fatiguing labors of the hand-mill. There had also been brought to the country several lots of goods, mostly taken to Cincinnati, the headquarters of military operation. Among the goods brought on were some articles essentially necessary for the comfort and health of the citizens. Their wearing apparel, bed clothing, etc., brought with them to the country, were worn out, and in the country there were neither wool, cotton or flannel to make more. So that the opportunity of obtaining supplies was very convenient to those who had the means to purchase with. Others had to supply themselves with the skin of the deer from the woods, which they dressed for clothing. While some resorted to the coarse lint of the nettle weed, from which they made a very rough substitute for linen.

The most important event which occurred during the winter was the fitting out of another expedition to go to St. Clair's battle-ground and bring the dead. A rumor was circulated among the people that some hunters had ventured out as far as the field of slaughter, and had seen the buzzards, panthers, wolves and wildcats tearing out the eyes and glutting themselves on the flesh of the dead men, and, although no one could tell the origin of the rumor, it produced an intense excitement, and public opinion called for the burial. The governor himself first visited Columbia to raise volunteers; but he, like all other generals who had been so unfortunate as to lose a battle, was unpopular with the militia and could not succeed. Saturday, of the following week, which was muster day for training the militia, General Wilkinson visited Columbia and attended the muster of the three companies, who all met at one place, on the bank of the river, in the center of the population. These three companies were then commanded by Captain Kibbey, successor to Captain

Gano, who had been promoted to major, and Captains Flinn and Hall. Like other boys, I was fond of visiting such places, and was present. After the men were paraded, General Wilkinson appeared, with his hunting shirt, moccasins, belt, knife and tomahawk—a real woodman's dress. He commenced by inspecting their guns, powder-horns and bullet bags, to learn what their supply of powder and balls was, occasionally tapping a man on the shoulder, saying: ''I see by the look of your eye you intend to go with me.'' After a most excellent and eloquent appeal to the feelings of the men, he asked them if they were willing that their brethren in arms, who had fallen in defense of their wives, children and firesides, should be eaten by the wild animals then glutting themselves on the slain in battle without a burying; and said, in a few minutes he would give an opportunity for all who were willing to go to manifest it by volunteering their services. At the proper time he gave orders, for all who intended to go with him, at the word ''forward march'' to step three paces forward. When the order was given, it was said that every healthy man in the three companies advanced three paces, and some who did not belong to the militia offered their services. After some directions were given them how they should prepare themselves, and when and where they should rendezvous, they were dismissed to give them time to prepare. That night, Sabbath and Sabbath night, were busily employed in making the preparations. Monday morning they left for Ft. Washington, from whence they took up the line of march and proceeded on the campaign, and were permitted, without being disturbed by the Indians, to prosecute their designs and bury the dead; and, after a short time, they returned without the loss of a man. On their return they erected another fort about halfway between Ft. Jefferson and Ft. Hamilton, to which General Wilkinson gave the name of Ft. St. Clair.

The result of the campaign, in a great measure, checked emigration, discouraged the citizens, and brought upon the infant settlement a train of evils by emboldening the Indians to venture into the very heart of all the new settlements, who were unchecked in their bloodshed by another army for near two years. During which time many citizens were slain, of which I will give you some account hereafter.

Yours truly,   E. F.

Lawrenceburg, March 25, 1851.

LETTER XVII.

MR. TORBET—In carrying my recollections back to the close of the year 1791, and the commencement of 1792, located, as I then was, in the midst of a population so deeply interested as the citizens of the Miami country were at that time, in every movement having for its object the driving back the Indians, I can not but feel astonished at the fortitude with which they bore the disappointment they felt at the result of St. Clair's defeat. It is true, they were somewhat cast down, but not in despair; and when the inquiry was made (as it often was), "What shall we do?" the answer was at hand: "We must breast the storm, and be prepared for every emergency." The minds of the people seemed to be prepared for the crisis, and notwithstanding all the discouragements thrown in their way they anticipated a final triumph. Among those most instrumental in keeping their hopes alive, if any one man deserves more praise than another, the highest honor was due to Captain Kibbey, who, by his vigilance in watching the movements of the Indians, and perseverance in pursuing after, and punishing them, when found hovering about our frontiers, gave a confidence in his bravery and skill that partly scattered the dark and gloomy cloud that was hanging over the country.

The first outbreak in the spring of '92, as far as my recollection serves me, was an attack upon a fatigue party sent out from Fort Jefferson, to perform some labor not far distant from the fort. While engaged in the labor assigned them they were taken by surprise and nearly all cut off, among them some valuable officers.

But the most important movement that year was an attempt at a negotiation for peace with the Indian tribes before resort was had to another campaign. To effect that object it was said that orders had been given to General St. Clair and General Wilkinson to select three men, to dispatch as commissioners to three of the most important tribes on our borders, to try, if possible, to restore the country to peace. Major Trueman, Colonel Hardin and Dr. Freeman were selected and commissioned for that purpose, and William Smalley, Joseph Gerrard and Thomas Flinn were employed to accompany them as guides and interpreters. Major Trueman also took with him a soldier by the name of William Lynch for a waiter; all of whom, after making the necessary arrangements about their business at home, and preparations for the hazardous adventure, left home on the mission to which they had been designated; none of whom, except William Smalley, ever returned.

This unfortunate mission, with its results, as related by Mr. Smalley after his return, will be the subject of my next letter.

Yours truly, E. F.

Lawrenceburg, April 21, 1851.

LETTER XVIII.

MR. TORBET—In complying with my promise in my last letter, I find myself embarrassed with the fact that the history of the country, founded in part upon official documents, appears to contradict what I know to be true in relation to the hazardous mission in which Major Trueman and his associates were engaged. General Wilkinson says they were selected and sent out by him as the authorized agents of the government. This I believe to be true, connected with the fact that he was to consult with and act in the matter as an associate of Governor St. Clair. I am confident that neither Generals Harmar or Wayne, as stated by some historians, had anything to do in the matter, as Harmar had ceased to command and left the country before any orders for such a mission issued from the department, and Wayne had neither come into command, or to the country, until the unfortunate attempt at negotiation had proved itself an entire failure.

Another difficulty, growing out of the letters of General Wilkinson to the department, is his stating that Trueman, Freeman and Hardin were dispatched by him at different times, which, according to my recollection of the matter, can not be true, as I feel satisfied in my own mind that they all started at the same time. And, even admitting that I might be wrong in my recollection, I can not be mistaken in the narrative Mr. Smalley gave me of the whole affair after his return. Again, General Wilkinson, in his official letter, says nothing was ever heard of these unfortunate men, except some vague accounts collected from the Indians by Mr. May, whom he had directed to desert and go over to the Indians to ascertain, if possible, their fate. This, however, may be accounted for from the fact that Wilkinson wrote before Smalley's return. But how can it be possible that it should still

be said by historians that the fate of this party is still unknown, or none of them ever returned, when it is and has
been known to thousands that William Smalley did return;
that his accounts were settled and paid at the department,
and that he afterward lived with his family until extreme old
age; was a man of good reputation, and died in the Wabash
country four or five years past, and always seemed willing to
communicate freely to all with whom he conversed upon the
subject, all the circumstances relating to the whole affair?
From all the circumstances, I feel justified in saying that on
or about the 7th of April, 1792, Major Alexander Trueman,
with William Lynch as a waiter, and William Smalley as an
interpreter; Colonel Hardin, with Mr. Thomas Flinn as an
interpreter, and Dr. Isaac Freeman, with Mr. Joseph Gerrard
as an interpreter, left Columbia to visit several of the Indian
tribes bordering on our frontiers on a mission, having for its
ultimate object a treaty of peace, and that of these seven
persons, none save William Smalley ever returned, as far as
I ever knew or heard; and that William Smalley did return
about Christmas of the same year, a fact in which I can not
be mistaken, as I well recollect hearing the report of the guns
fired as a salute when he came home; of seeing and talking
with him, perhaps a thousand times after his return at his
own house and at other places; of his appearing before Major
William Goforth, a justice of the peace, at his request, and
there relating to him, in the presence of all who wished to attend, all the circumstances connected with his travels during
his absence, and the number of his companions, and of his
own captivity and escape, answering all the questions asked
him freely, except that he then declined relating the manner
in which his escape from captivity was effected, and that afterwards (say in 1811) he related to me (with a view to its pub-
lication, if I should think proper at any aftertime to publish
it) a narrative of all the circumstances connected with the

whole affair, which I will give next week if health permits, and which, in combination of facts bearing upon my mind in relation to the whole affair,' I fully believe is true.

Yours truly,

E. F.

Lawrenceburg, April 29, 1851.

LETTER XIX.

MR. TORBET—As promised in my last letter, I now send you a narrative of the mission of Major Alexander Trueman and others, to the several Indian tribes, to whom they were sent, related to me by Mr. William Smalley, the only survivor of the company sent out by the government. Some time in the year 1811 I visited Mr. Smalley's family, and was detained for a night. I asked Mr. Smalley to relate to me the circumstances that occurred during the trip he had with Major Trueman, on his attempted visit to the Indians, which he gave me, as near as I can recollect, in the following language, which, after returning home, I penned:

"On the 7th of April, 1792, we (meaning Major Trueman, Colonel Hardin, Dr. Freeman, Thomas Flinn, Joseph Gerrard, William Lynch and himself) started from Columbia, and in the most convenient manner we could struck on to Harmar's trace, which we followed until a change in the course made it necessary to leave it to pursue a more direct route to the towns to which we were sent. We continued to travel together in company, carrying with us a white flag, until about the middle of the afternoon of the eighth day of our travel, when a halt was called, and a consultation was held about the propriety of separating, that each of the commissioners might take a direct course to the town or tribe to which he was sent. It was the opinion of Mr. Flinn, Mr.

Gerrard, and myself, that we could not travel any longer together without some of the company going very much out of their course; so we parted. Major Trueman, William Lynch, and myself, took our course toward the Delaware towns, and about sunset met three Indians on the waters of a stream called Hog creek. We presented our flag, and I hailed them saying: 'We are on an errand of peace; the white people want to have peace, and have sent this man (meaning Major Trueman) to make proposals for peace': and proposed that we should camp and spend the night together; to which, after consulting among themselves a short time, they agreed. After making a fire, Major Trueman directed William Lynch, his waiter, to prepare some chocolate for supper; which he did, and Trueman invited the Indians to sup with him; to which they consented, and expressed a great fondness for the new kind of supper. After supper, as neither Trueman or Lynch could speak the Indian language, I entered into a conversation with them upon the subject of our visit, and attempted to show the advantage the Indians would gain by having a market for their furs on the Ohio river instead of Detroit. I told them the white people were anxious to have peace, and open a trade with them, and to exchange powder and lead with them for their meat, to all of which they listened, and appeared well pleased—occasionally asking me to make certain inquiries of my captain (meaning Major Trueman), which I did, and interpreted to them the answers. About 11 o'clock, as I supposed, Major Trueman, having a very bad cold, occasioning a severe cough, proposed to lie down, which I communicated to the Indians; on hearing which the oldest Indian said, 'Ask your captain if he will let one of his men be tied, as you are stronger than we are, not counting my boy (a lad about fourteen) and he is afraid to lie down'; to which Trueman replied he might tie Lynch. The Indian then went a little from the fire, and stripped the bark from some small hickory sprouts, with which he tied Lynch's arms above his elbows, fastening the bark across his back, but not so as to render it very inconvenient to him. Lynch then lay down back of the fire, and Trueman spread some bear skins on the ground in front, and lay down on them, covering himself with a blanket; I lay down on some bear skins with my head raised by placing my elbows on the ground, with one hand each side of my face, in such a posture as to have Trueman and the Indians before me; the latter still sitting up. In this position we entered into another conversation about the success they had had in hunting the past winter. The old Indian complained of having very bad luck, and said he believed it was partly owing to his gun-lock, at which moment he reached out his hand and took hold of the gun, and showed me that he had lost the screws that fastened the lock on, and had to tie it with a leather string. While he was showing his gun, and continuing his complaints, Major Trueman had a very severe spell of coughing, and as soon as the phlegm seemed to rise turned his head over to spit when the Indian shot him, the ball entering about the point of the shoulder-blade and passing out near the nipple on the opposite side, which killed him instantly; so that he did not turn his head back. I sprang up in a moment and ran for the woods, and when, as I suppose, I was about two rods from the fire the other Indian shot at me, but without effect. The Indian boy, like myself, made for the woods, and the old Indian, who first shot, ran back of the fire and seized Lynch, who had raised to his feet and got partially untied, and hallooed to the other Indian to help him, saying: ' This man is stronger than I am, and will get untied and escape'; at which call he went round and struck him on his head with a tomahawk several times. During this time I remained stationary, reflecting on what I should do. I felt as though the joints of my loins were loosed, my knees were knocking together, and teeth rattling. I felt as though to escape was impossible. I was eight days travel from home, had no gun to kill game with to subsist on, and should have to lie by in daylight and travel at night, so that I must starve before I could get home. I concluded I was in the hands of God, and must submit to my fate, and in an instant became composed. After a short time the old Indian called to me, and told me to come to the fire. I refused, saying, 'You will kill me'; to which he replied, 'We will not.' I told him he had promised not to hurt the other men; to which he replied, 'I wanted his gun.' After further conversation, knowing they had not loaded their guns, I placed my butcher-knife in a concealed position, so that I could use it if necessary, and told them if they would put their guns and tomahawks out of reach I would return to the fire; which they did. I then advanced about half way to the fire and halted—the Indian still urging me to come to the fire; I told him if they would sit down I would; they then sat down, and I went up to the fire. They requested me to sit down, which I did.'' And there he said he passed such a gloomy night that a house full of gold would not be a temptation to go through another such, and continued his narrative.

Not to make this number too long, I must defer the balance for another.   Yours truly,   E. F.

Lawrenceburg, May 5, 1851.

LETTER XX.

MR. TORBET—I now proceed with the narrative where I left off in my last.

"I began," said Mr. Smalley, "to reflect on myself for consenting to accompany him on so hazardous a business, knowing, as I believe I did, and as I often told Major Trueman, that we should all be killed. But the fear of being called a coward had spurred me on, to leave for the time my wife and children and home, to throw away my life, merely to escape the reproach that I feared would follow a refusal to go. I next began to charge my misfortunes on the president and congress, and wished, for the moment, they were all with me to share my fate, and lastly, I reproached the society of Friends, who, I understood, had petitioned to congress to make an attempt at negotiation before sending out another army to fight them. I then again concluded all these movements were directed by an overruling Providence, and it was my place to submit, and that, trusting in Him, I might yet be preserved and restored to my family. I concluded that, prepared, as I was, with a knife, I should be able to kill one, and possibly both, and, in the latter case, could have the advantage of the provisions we had with us, and a gun and ammunition, as well as of a pony Major Trueman had brought along to pack his baggage on, so as to render it probable to make my way back to Columbia. I also took into consideration how far I would be justifiable, as a professed Christian, as a last resort to save my life, to deceive them by making false statements about my intentions in coming among them. I thought of my relation to God and to the Baptist Church, as a member with them, and came to the conclusion that neither God nor the church would condemn me for such resort, when impelled to it by the most urgent necessity. I then commenced telling them I was sorry they had killed these men, not that I cared anything about them, but because I wished the Indians well, for whom I had more friendship than for the white people, and thought it would be for their best interest to have peace. I told them I had been raised among their tribe, been adopted into one of their families, and when I left them had an Indian father and brother whom I loved, and that I left them by consent, with the privilege of remaining among the white people or returning to them, as I should choose; that I engaged to do an errand for them at Pittsburg (then called Ft. Duquesne), after which I visited George's creek, the place where I was captured by the Indians when a boy. I told them on my arrival at that place, my friends were all dead or gone, and that from that time I had determined to return to the Indians, and had embraced the opportunity of accompanying these men, as the first ever offered, by which I could elude the watchfulness of the white people, who were always jealous of me as being more friendly to the Indians than to them. I told them if I could find my Indian father or brother, they would confirm all I had said upon the subject. While we were engaged in talking, as above stated, the Indian boy returned from the woods, when the old Indian told him to kill that man behind the fire, '' for he disturbs me with his groanings;'' adding, '' it is very disagreeable to me to hear him;'' upon which order the boy immediately killed him by striking him on the head. He then bid the boy scalp him, which he did, and brought the scalp to the Indian, who threw it at me, and told me to dress it, which, with me, was the most trying and terrifying event attending the whole scene. I had to brace up my nerves so as to show no regret, or else I should expose to them the falsity of all I had said, which seemed to require more courage than I had. Several times I found myself drawing my arm, and preparing my mind to plunge my knife into the vitals of one of them, when again I was checked by the consideration that to me it would be immediate death; so that with a mind changing with almost every breath, I passed one of the most gloomy nights that was ever witnessed by man, through which I must have been overwhelmed, had it not been for the help of God and the encouragement given me by the repeated and positive pledges of the Indians that I should not be hurt, until delivered up to the Indian chief next morning, at the town where he resided, which promise they fulfilled, and the next morning conducted me safe to the town, and delivered me into the hands of Boconjehaulis, the principal chief of that tribe, who had me placed under the guard of a number of warriors until further orders.''

Finding I can not condense so as to give the transactions before the chief, without tasking the reader with too long a letter, I defer that for another number.

Yours truly,   E. F.

Lawrenceburg, May 12, 1851.

LETTER XXI.

Mr. Torbet—Mr. Smalley continued: '' After being detained a short time by my guard, I was ordered to appear again before Boconjehaulis, who was then considered by the Indians their king. Assuming a rather pompous attitude, he asked me in a very stern way what I had come there for, to which I replied, 'To live with the Indians.' He then inquired, 'And what did these men with you come for?' To which I answered, 'To try to make peace,' they said. 'I think,' said he, 'they were very impudent to attempt to come here; I had given them no leave to come.' In answer . I said, 'I do not know anything about it, only what they said; but they told me if I would come with them, as a pilot and interpreter, I might stay with the Indians; and that was all I knew about it.' I then repeated what I had told the Indians in the camp the night before about my Indian father and brother, calling them by name, and rehearsed the circumstances of my captivity and adoption into the family, and of my leaving them with the privilege of remaining with the white people, or returning to them as I might choose, declared my intention of now remaining with them, and repeated the statements I had made of having no relations or friends among the white people. After I had concluded, an Indian rose up in the crowd, and said he knew both the men I had claimed as my father and brother, and knew where they now lived, not more than between one and two days travel off. I requested to have them sent for, to which the king consented, and I prevailed on the Indian to go after them, who started immediately, and I was returned to the care of my guard. During the absence of the Indian I had sent for my father, I was brought each day before the king, and, as I thought, examined to try to make me contradict myself; consequently, I was very careful to repeat, in the same words, my friendship to the Indians, and reasons for returning to live with them again. The second day of my captivity, I saw, at a distance, the head of a white man, brought into the town by some Indians, elevated on a pole, which I believed was the head of Mr. Joseph Gerrard, who had accompanied Dr. Freeman. But as I had not told the Indians of any other company besides Trueman, Lynch and myself, I dare not show an anxiety about Mr. Gerrard, lest I should betray myself, and did not ascertain to a certainty, but believe it was Mr. Gerrard's head, and am the more confirmed in it now, as he was never afterward heard of by me. I was detained in a very restless state of suspense until the arrival of my Indian father and brother, with the return of the Indian I had sent after them, who interested themselves as much for me as any natural father could have done—attending me every day when examined by the king, continually pleading my cause for me, and confirming all I had said about my former residence with them, and the circumstances connected with my return to the white people. I was detained fourteen days as a prisoner, and examined each day about my professed attachment to the In-

20

dians, when I was given up to my Indian father, on his be-
coming responsible for my conduct, and submission to the
chief of the town where I was going to reside with him.
Being in part relieved from my anxiety about my own personal
safety, I set out immediately to accompany my Indian father
home.   But new difficulties presented themselves to my mind.
My most faithful father and friend had involved himself so
far for me as to endanger his life if I should escape without
leave of the chief, and I was still kept at a distance from my wife
and children, and could devise no means to communicate to
them my situation, without having the false statements I made
to the Indians exposed; which I knew would cost me my life.
While reflecting in my own mind about these difficulties, and
suffering from the anxiety I felt about my family, I saw, at a
distance, Mr. Patrick Moor brought in as a prisoner, only
thirteen days from Columbia.   This increased my alarm, for
I feared he might say something about my family before I
could see him, or that should I meet him in the presence of
the Indians, he might speak of my wife and children.   No
person unacquainted with my situation can imagine how I
felt; an old acquaintance near at hand, who I knew could
tell me about my beloved family, from whom I had been so
long separated, and yet I dare not approach him.   I then
concluded if I was at home again the world would be no temptation to draw me into the difficulties I was then involved in.
Providence, however, so overruled matters that I again
escaped; had an interview with Moor—heard from home—
but had no opportunity to communicate to my wife the fact
that I was still living.   In the midst of my anxiety I made
known to my adopted father that I had a wife and children
at Columbia, and wanted to return to them, who, without
hesitation, promised me all the aid he could give.   'It will
not do,' said he, 'to attempt it now, but we will watch for
an opportunity more favorable, and as soon as it can be done

without endangering your life, and my own, I will assist you to return.

Finding my letter will be too long if I follow up the narrative to his return, I defer the balance for another number.

Yours truly,   E. F.

Lawrenceburg, May 19, 1851.

LETTER XXII.

MR. TORBET—I will now present your readers with the escape of Mr. Smalley from the Indians, and his return to his family. He continued:

"I remained in a state of painful anxiety about my family and home, and often conversed with my Indian father upon the subject, who, after due consideration, made the following proposal: 'That we should obtain from the chief of the village permission to go out upon a hunting tour, and while absent I should desert and make the best of the way I could home.' In pursuance of that plan, he applied to the chief, who readily granted his request, but required us to return at night, which we did, as it was thought one day would not give me a sufficient advantage of time to make sure work in eluding their pursuit. During the summer similar applications were made and granted by the chief, who still restricted us to only one day's absence, which we always complied with in the most punctual manner. In the fall, when the weather began to be somewhat cold, we made application for permission to be absent three days, urging as a reason that the game was so scarce near the village that we could expect but little success in hunting unless permitted to go farther in the woods than we could do in one day and return at night; this request, appearing reasonable, was granted, and we went out and returned accordingly. While out on the three days' tour we made the final arrangement for my return home, as follows:

"We concluded to make application for a fall hunt, to be absent eight days, and should we succeed in obtaining permission, my Indian father and brother agreed to accompany me seven days in a direction towards Columbia, where we were to part, and I was to make my way home and they return and report that I had deserted; and as an excuse for their long absence, to say they had pursued after me as long as they dare venture, on account of their near approach to the settlement of the white people, and in that manner conceal from the Indians my escape until I could reach home. We succeeded in our application, and set out on our journey, and my mind was elated with the prospect of reaching home in a few days; but, unfortunately, the first night my prospects, for the time being, were blasted by my Indian brother being attacked with a most distressing pain in his hip, shooting down to the knees, which proved to be a white swelling, and rendered him unable to travel. Being detained several days in the woods taking care of him (for I felt my obligation binding on me too strong to be broken off), we concluded to try and remove him to the lake shore, where there was a Frenchman from Canada living, from which place I could have an opportunity to escape across the lake. By great exertions we succeeded in reaching the Frenchman's house, where we had again to make an appeal to a stranger to aid me in an attempt to cross the lake. My Indian father approached him by asking him if he could confide in him without fear of being betrayed, to which he answered he could. He then said to the Frenchman, 'this man' (meaning me) 'is a prisoner, and has a wife and children at home, and wants to return to them, and we are trying to help him into Canada.' To which the Frenchman replied, 'I dare not help him, for the Indians would kill me, but,' pointing to the shore, he said, 'there is a canoe that belongs to me, but I dare not assist him.' He was then asked how we could pay for the canoe, to which answer he replied by asking, 'can your white man make an ox yoke'? On being told he could, 'I want a yoke,' said he, 'and there is the canoe, but I dare not sell it to him.' We understood him, and I made him a yoke. We afterward concluded it would not do to cross the lake in, as it could not ride the waves if there should be a storm. We again changed our plan, and I concluded to make my way along the lake shore to Preskiel in Pennsylvania. This plan being settled on, my Indian father said to me: 'I will go up the lake to find a suitable place to make a camp for hunting, and leave you to take care of my son, and if while I am gone you should take the canoe and go off, we can say I was absent, and my son was so lame he could not follow you, so that they could not attach any blame to either of us.' Accordingly he went to the woods, and I, after procuring some bread and meat, took possession of the canoe without leave, and steered my course for Preskiel (Presque Isle, now Erie), Pennsylvania. After a few days' paddling my canoe a part of the way along the lake shore, and walking through the woods, I reached my native state, and once more enjoyed the inexpressible happiness of being again in civilized society. From Preskiel I made my way through the wilderness across to the waters of the Allegheny, and down that river to Pittsburgh, thence down the Ohio to Columbia, where I was once more permitted to meet my old neighbors, who, when they saw me coming, appeared so overcome with surprise and gladness that they ran out to meet me from every direction, and take me by the hand to welcome my return, partially obstructing or retarding my way to my family, so that I had almost to force my way through the crowd to my own dwelling, where I found my beloved wife and children in good health, who were overjoyed to receive me, as one who had returned from the grave. Others may imagine, to some extent, but can not realize, the joy I felt in finding myself once more in the bosom of my family— by my own fireside—and my thankfulness to that kind Providence that had watched over my path, and again brought me home in peace, after an absence of eight months and twenty-three days, in time to spend the holidays with those whose happiness and welfare had created so much solicitude in my own breast during my absence, and who had never heard from me from the time I took them by the hand and bid them farewell.''

I have now given the substance of the narrative as related to me by Mr. Smalley, and have the utmost confidence in the correctness of what he said. I wish, however, to have it understood that it was a verbal communication, and not penned until some time after; also that I have abridged his statements considerably. And here, permit me to say that although Messrs. Gerrard and Flinn never returned to their families, their memory should be equally cherished by the pioneers of the west as patriots who sacrificed their lives upon the altar of their country, and, had a favorable result followed their adventures, they would have shared in the benefits since enjoyed by those hardy sons who risked their all to settle this goodly land.   Yours truly,   E. F.

Lawrenceburg, May 26, 1851.

LETTER XXIII.

MR. TORBET—In the spring of 1792, the inhabitants of the new settlements were again reduced to a very scanty allowance of bread, most of them having exhausted their crop of corn in the winter; and for meat they were entirely dependent on the game in the woods, which was brought in daily by the hunters. To show the dangers the hunters were exposed to, and the uncertainty of regular supplies, I will relate the following facts:

Mr. Patrick Moor, a young man from Ireland, who had made his way to the new settlement in the west, undertook the business of hunting and killing meat. One morning, he went out as usual, in search of game, but returned no more for more than twenty years; nor was he heard from during that time, so far as I know, except the account given by Mr. Smalley after his return Mr. Moor gave the following account of his captivity:

"I was," he said, "passing through the woods in search of game, when suddenly I was surprised by the report of a gun, shot at me by some Indians, the ball of which passed through my side, but gave me only a flesh wound. I immediately turned towards home, and exerted myself to escape; and for a time thought I should succeed, being about thirty yards ahead of my pursuers. I kept my distance very well, until I came to a long tree, which had fallen. In attempting to cross it, the Indians gained some advantage of me in distance, but the Indians, like myself, being very much exhausted by the chase, the first one who attempted to cross the log, fell back, whereupon, seeing their leader fall, one ran round one end of the tree; seeing that move, I wheeled immediately off, and ran for the other end, so that while they were running round the tree, I gained so much on them that they gave up the pursuit and stopped. Being very much exhausted when I saw them stop, I did the same to collect a little air in my lungs; but at that unfortunate moment my hopes were all ended by seeing three Indians in advance of me, who were waiting for me to come up to them. I knew that, fresh as they were, I could not get out of their way, and surrendered myself as their prisoner. The Indians who had at first shot and pursued me, came up and claimed me as their prisoner, saying, ' if they had not run me down the others could not have taken me;' to which the others replied, 'You had given up the pursuit, and had it not been for us he would have escaped.' Both parties were very stubborn, and in their quarrel came very near taking my life. One Indian raised his tomahawk to strike it in my head, and thus put an end to the quarrel; but the other knocked it off with his hand, and said, ' Take him, we will not kill a prisoner;' so I escaped death, and was carried off a captive."

The same summer, Mr. Francis Griffin started for Lexington, Ky., to procure corn for his family, and a few days after was found dead, lying on his face with the blade of a war club sticking in his flesh between his shoulders, which was all that was ever heard about the way he came to his death.

Thus, the inhabitants had to learn "that in life they were in the midst of death."   Yours truly,   E. F.

Lawrenceburg, June 2, 1851.

———

LETTER XXIV.

Mr. TORBET—As, in my last letter, I related two circumstances to show the extreme danger the inhabitants of the new settlements were exposed to, when they ventured abroad in search of bread and meat, I will now give you a fact, to show how insecure they were at home.

In the winter of 1791–2, there were a few families ventured to form a settlement at the upper (or north) end of Turkey bottom, so as to be nearer their work in tending their cornfields in the bottom. For their security, they built a small fortification, consisting of a block-house with pickets around the door, to which they might retreat, in case of an attack from the Indians. Among these families there was one by the name of Gordon, in which there was a boy named James, perhaps fourteen years old, and a younger daughter whom they called Nancy. During the season of making sugar, Mr. Gordon tapped some trees on the side hill to obtain sugar water for the use of his family; but the weather being rather too cold the trees produced but little water, and that, in the night, froze nearly solid, leaving a small quantity of water in the middle of the ice, very sweet. One Sunday, James and Nancy invited a boy named John Webb to go with them and get some sweet sugar water; to which young Webb replied, "That his mother had told him he must not run about or play on the Sabbath day; "but, on being told by James, "she would never know it," he started with them, having about forty rods to go; but about half way of the distance he said "a thought came into his mind that he ought not to disobey his mother, if she did not know it," and he turned back and left them, but James and Nancy went on. On arriving among the sugar trees, they each selected a trough, broke the ice, and bent over to drink the sweet water. While in the act of drinking some Indians approached suddenly, and one Indian advanced toward each of them. Nancy was taken prisoner, and carried into captivity as was supposed, and never more heard from by her parents. But James, seeing the Indian coming toward him, ran for the fort. He said, in the race (the Indian being close in his rear), he saw no way of escape but by leaping a sapling that was bent over his path too low to run under; and he concluded if he could get the foot foremost that he commonly started to jump on he could leap it—the Indian being in his rear, with his arms spread to grasp him, when he should come up to the sapling. James, however, succeeded in making his leap, and the Indian being bent forward, with his arms spread to lay hold of him, not expecting he could pass over, struck the little tree so hard with his breast that it knocked him back, and he fell on the ground, and James made his way to the fort.

Mr. Webb is still living, and ranks among the most respectable farmers of Hamilton county, and no doubt remembers better than any other his narrow escape, by honoring the instructions of his mother, not to desecrate the Sabbath day.

Yours truly,   E. F.

Lawrenceburg, June 7, 1851.

LETTER XXV.

MR. TORBET—After the almost annihilation of St. Clair's army in November, 1791, and the discharge of the Kentucky militia, the country was left nearly without means of defense, and the Indians seemed to have come to the conclusion that they might, with impunity, hover round our settlements, as there were very few soldiers to pursue after them, and as there was, as yet, but little talk of another army until the result of the trial at negotiation with the Indian tribes should be certainly known. From the foregoing causes the settlements were continually annoyed with marauding parties, stealing their horses, and killing or carrying off the inhabitants into captivity. We had frequent reports of murders by the Indians at North Bend, Cincinnati, and other out stations; but, as I was small and lived at a distance from the scene of action, I can not recollect the names. I remember a man being killed in the vicinity of Cincinnati, on the west of Mill creek, while hunting his cows, on one Sunday morning, and another while choping cord-wood in the back part of the town, between the Hamilton road and Mill creek, and, at another time, a man was driven from his team while plowing a lot not far from where the center of the city now is, and his horses were cut loose and taken off. In the same year a Mr. Van Hyse was taken prisoner by the Indians. He, however, was not detained long before he returned, and it was believed among the people that in consequence of the kind treatment the Indians heretofore spoken of received when prisoners, that Mr. Van Hyse was very much favored, as he resided in that place when at home. Of these difficulties I heard as a boy, and being at a distance, was not so deeply affected by them. I, however, proceed to give an account of a most melancholy event that occurred partly under my own notice, being in the daily habit of seeing the sufferers before they went out.

Mr. William Lytle, then of Kentucky, afterward Gen. Lytle, of Cincinnati, visited Columbia to employ some men to accompany him in an exploring tour on the Virginia military county lands, east of the Little Miami, to find where he could locate some land warrants to the best advantage. Among others, he engaged Benjamin Alcott, James Newel and Henry Ball, three respectable young men, to accompany him on horseback, who were to meet him next day at Covalt's station, a small settlement about twelve miles above Columbia, on the Little Miami. Thinking it would be safer, these young men concluded they would not leave home until near night, so that when they should have to pass the narrows on the river below Round Bottom it would be dark, and by riding fast they would be exposed to less danger, that being considered the most dangerous place on the way. According to arrangements, they started a little while before night, but had traveled but about three miles, when crossing the point of a ridge between two small ravines, near where Madisonville now stands, they were fired at by the Indians. Mr. Alcott was wounded in the arm, but remained on his horse, but both Newel and Ball fell to the ground. Alcott wheeled his horse, and the other two horses followed him, I recollect being out with a number of boys playing, when suddenly our attention was arrested by the noise of the horses advancing in full speed. Those that had lost their riders seemed to be trying to escape with the same speed as the others. As they passed our little crowd, Mr. Alcott cried out, "Run home, the Indians are coming; I am wounded, and Newel and Ball are killed or taken prisoners." We all hastened home to tell the news. The alarm was spread, and by morning a party of the militia were ready to start in search of the missing. They soon reached the fatal spot, and found Newel still living, but most horribly and barbarously mangled, but could not find Ball. Newel was brought into his widowed mother, brother and sisters, a melancholy object to fix the eye upon. The whole hairy scalp of his head was taken off, and several strokes of a tomahawk had passed through his skull into the brain, A surgeon was sent for, who attended, but said, "it would be in vain to attempt to do anything, as he could not possibly survive his wound." He lingered through most of the day and died. On examination, it was found that his gunshot wound was but a slight one. Mr. Newel was not able, after being found, to give an account of this sad affair.

Many years afterward Mr. Ball returned, and gave an account of the whole transaction. He said they were riding in a brisk trot, when they were unexpectedly fired on by a number of Indians; that Mr. Newel was slightly wounded and fell from his horse; that they shot at him and missed, but his horse wheeled about so suddenly that the girth of his saddle broke, and he fell with the saddle, and made an attempt to escape, but had not more than got on his feet before he was seized hold of by some Indians, who, perceiving that Newel was wounded, did not give any attention to him until they had him (Ball) tied. They then began to search for Newel, but he was gone, and as it was now nearly dark, they started off without finding him; but after traveling a few rods they saw Newel's dog standing and looking up a small bushy topped tree. They at first passed by it, but after going a few rods further, one of the Indians said, "The white man must be up that tree, or the dog would not be there whining," on which suggestion they returned and got Newel down, but as he was too badly wounded to travel well, they scalped and tomahawked him.

Soon after this sad affair, rumors were afloat that another army was coming, to be commanded by Gen. Wayne, which gave great encouragement that they would be relieved from the almost continued encroachments of the Indians.

Yours truly,   E. F.

Lawrenceburg, June 17, 1851.

LETTER XXVI.

MR. TORBET—I fear I shall weary the patience of the reader by the monotony there is in so many Indian tales following each other.

Shortly after the death of Mr. Newel, as related in my last letter, it was generally supposed that the Indians had retired from our frontiers to attend to their crops at home, and as fur skins and meat killed in the woods in warm weather were of but little value, consequently there was but little inducement to stay where they could do nothing but hunt. The inhabitants, generally, were permitted to pursue their business through the spring and summer with but little difficulty from the Indians. They, however, this season, suffered very much from the destructions of the cut-worm, which, for a time, seemed to shut out all prospect of a crop, except in ground worked for the first time that season. The approach of hot weather, however, subdued them, and by replanting there was something more than half a crop of corn; but a considerable portion did not get ripe, which caused a scarcity again the ensuing spring equal almost to any former time.

Rumors were frequently heard during this season of military preparations being made to drive the Indians back. Wayne, it was said, was coming, and at his presence it was supposed the Indians would flee. The movements of the army were tardy, and they remained at Legionville, near Pittsburg, that winter. Early in the fall it was reported that the Indians were again on our frontiers, and that it was dangerous for the white people to venture far from home. They, however, did very little mischief in the early part of the season, and it was supposed their object was to hunt; but towards spring they became more troublesome, and occasionally stole horses from the white people. In the latter part of the winter there were some young men about Gerrard station, on the east of the Miami, who concluded to play what they called a "trick" on them, as horses were their object. They accordingly took a white horse from a drove of poor, worn-out pack-horses that belonged to the contractor, and had been sent there to recruit in the woods, as they could neither buy hay nor corn, and hoppled him near to a place where three large trees had blown down and fallen across each other, so as to make three sides of a pen; and after they had hoppled and cross-hoppled the poor horse, so that he could not move, they put a bell on him, and concealed themselves behind the fallen trees. They had not been long concealed before they saw an Indian advancing towards the horse. It being very bright moonlight, his first move was to stop the clattering of the bell, which he did by stuffing it with dry leaves. He then bent down on his knees to untie the hopples, when the boys shot at him, and he fell on his face, but immediately arose to his feet and ran. They dare not follow after him that night, fearing there might be more Indians near at hand. But in the morning early they went to the place, and found that he had bled profusely, and had left his gun behind. They followed his tracks a few miles, and came to a camp in the woods, where, they supposed, about five Indians had been staying for a length of time; but they were all gone, and the pack of one was left behind with some bloody clothes. From that time the people about Gerrard station were upon the lookout—expecting the Indians would retaliate.

In the spring of that year three families had settled in small cabins on the bank of the Ohio river, about a half mile from the station, above the mouth of the Miami, near to each other. The name of one family was Raridon, one Reynolds and one Smith. Early in March, one evening after they had barred their doors, one of the small boys, with a good deal of surprise, cried out, " There is an Indian looking down the chimney." All about the fire immediately looked up, but saw no Indian. They then commenced expressing an opinion whether the boy had seen an Indian, some thinking one way and some the other; but all concluded it was best to stay in the house and keep the doors shut. The next day the people at the station were notified of what the boy said, but they generally concluded he was mistaken. The following evening Mr. James Welch, who was making sugar in his house, and gathering his water from trees on a side-hill near at hand, went up the side-hill after water between sundown and dark, followed by a little dog, but had been gone but a few minutes before the dog returned apparently very much alarmed. He turned round from the house, looked up the hill and barked as though greatly distressed. Mrs. Welch commenced calling Welch, but obtained no answer. She continued calling louder and louder, until she became almost frantic. The neighbors ran together, and concluded he was either killed or taken prisoner, but that it would not be safe to follow after him before morning. In the morning they assembled together, and went in search and soon found the buckets, but found nothing of Welch. All they knew about him afterwards, until his return, was mere conjecture. Some time in October or November following, Welch returned and gave an account of his captivity. He said as he was passing up the hill he was seized by three Indians, one to each arm, and another behind him, with a tomahawk in his hand, and marched immediately off six or eight miles to an Indian camp, where there were twenty-five or thirty warriors awaiting the return of the three men who had captured him. He learned that they were about making an attack on the three families on the bank of the Ohio, and had sent some spies down the night before to ascertain how many men there were in the three houses; that the spies had returned and reported, and also reported that one of them had been discovered by a boy, and related the talk that had taken place in the house growing out of what the boy had said, and said that he had laid still on the roof until the people in the house went to sleep, and had then crawled down. On hearing this reported, they had sent three men to learn whether the boy's story had created any alarm, with the intention, if it did not, to make the attack in the after part of the night. These men reported that there was no alarm among the people; that they were all at home pursuing their usual business, and how they had taken Welch. Their first conclusion was to kill him and make the attack, but as soon as this conclusion was announced an old Indian arose, saying, ''You are wrong; there's an alarm now; you have taken this man and now they are all alarmed, and will be ready for you; they ought not to have disturbed this man.'' They then tried the question over, and determined it would be best to make their way home, and immediately shouldered their sacks and were off, taking Welch with them as a prisoner, and kept him through the summer to raise corn, and treated him to about the same fare with themselves. In the fall he fell in company with a Canadian who had come among the Indians to buy furs, and had a boat up one of the rivers to convey them across the lake. Welch made a bargain with him to meet at the last point of high land before entering the lake, from which place the Canadian agreed to take him across the lake. Welch succeeded in taking an Indian canoe and passing down the river. Though he was discovered and closely pursued, yet he eluded their pursuit by running his canoe into the bullrushes and hiding himself in the grass, and finally got into the Canadian's boat, who hid him under some furs until next morning and took him over into Canada, from whence he made his way home. Mr. Welch had not been heard from from the time he was taken prisoner until they saw him coming home, where he found his family all in good health, and glad to see him.   Yours truly,   E. F.

Lawrenceburg, June 24, 1851.

LETTER XXVII.

MR. TORBET—In carrying out my designs in writing a series of letters containing some historical sketches attending the first settlement of the Miami country, I can not (though tired of relating Indian stories) pass by the following lamentable circumstance as being one that affected me more than any other during the war. Mr. O. M. Spencer, one of the sufferers, lived in the same place with myself. We were about the same age, and had been to school together. In addition, I heard the lamentations of his father and mother over their lost son in the day of their affliction, and, though a boy, I could not but sympathize with them.

About the 3d of July, 1792, some officers from Fort

21

Washington visited Columbia in a keel-boat rowed by sol-diers. As was usual with all the officers of the army, they called on Colonel Spencer, and, while there, invited his daughters to accompany them to Fort Washington to attend a Fourth of July celebration to take place the next day, promising to see them safe home on the 5th. By consent of their father and mother they accepted the invitation, and their brother Oliver was permitted to accompany them. On the 5th, they made the necessary preparations to return, but Oliver was missing, having wandered off with some boys he had fallen in company with. After waiting as long as they could for his return, without making it too late to row the boat to Columbia and back that night, they started and left him behind. When Oliver found he was left, he was very uneasy, as he said his father had enjoined it on him very strictly to return with his sisters; and he sought an oppor-tunity to go home with other company, and finally found a canoe belonging to (or in possession of) two men by the name of Light and Layton, who had gone down to Cincinnati that morning, taking with them a Mrs. Coleman, who had some marketing to sell to the soldiers. He made applica-tioɲ, and was permitted to return with them. On his way up, he complained of being so cramped by the way he had to sit in the canoe that he asked permission to get out and walk a part of the way, which they allowed him to do. About a mile below Crawfish they were attacked by the Indians, and Light and Layton were both shot—the former wounded, and the latter killed instantly; both fell and turned the canoe over, and, with Mrs. Coleman, were all thrown into the river, and young Spencer was taken captive. Some person at Columbia heard the guns and saw the men fall, so that the alarm was given immediately that the Indians had killed a canoe-load of people coming up the river below Columbia. The militia, who were always on the alert, ran for their guns, and, without waiting for orders, repaired to the spot as quickly as possible. On arriving at the place, they found Light and Layton in the river where the canoe had upset (the water being shoal), and Mrs. Coleman a short distance below holding on to a snag. They took them out of the river, found Layton dead, Light wounded in the arm, and Mrs. Coleman unhurt. Light and Mrs. Coleman remained in the water thinking it would be more safe, as they did not know but the Indians might still be lurking in the woods. Mrs. Coleman said she got hold of the snag, and turned her eyes toward the Indians before they had taken young Spencer; that he did not try to escape, but that when the Indians came up to him he clasped his hands and drew them over his head; that they did not hurt him as long as she could see him, but led him in great haste up the bank to the woods, and that she saw but two Indians. Colonel Spencer himself was on the ground, of course greatly distressed, but very much composed, considering the circumstances he was placed in. Several of the militia volunteered to pursue immediately after the Indians, and recapture Oliver if possible, but the colonel objected. He said, "If they have determined to keep him prisoner, he may some day return; but if pursued and overtaken, their first object will be to kill him, then run;" so that it was concluded best not to pursue after them. This circumstance created great alarm. It had hitherto been considered that there was little or no danger that season of the year, as the Indians were generally at home tending to their crops. And it was also thought that as Cincinnati had now grown to be more populous than Columbia was, and that as there were so many soldiers about, the Indians would hardly dare venture between the two places. I recollect the Sunday following, as the people were collecting for worship at the meeting-house on the point of the hill, some neighbors, meeting Colonel Spencer, began to condole with him on account of his loss, to which, with deep emotion, he commenced a reply by complaining of the suspense in which his mind was held. "My oldest son," said he, "left home, leaving a wife and one infant son behind, to make a voyage at sea, and we never heard from him again; and now my youngest and only remaining son is either slain or captive among the savages. It would be some relief to know what his fate has been;" and, as if overcome with grief, he could say no more. The narrative of O. M. Spencer's captivity, treatment, and final return, as published by himself, renders it unnecessary that I should say anything further up on the subject.

The attention of all the inhabitants, from about this time, was taken up with speculation and rumors about the preparations that were then being made to raise a powerful army to be placed under the command of General Wayne, in whom, notwithstanding all their former disappointments, they had the most unshaken confidence. The last consideration, in part, made up for the gloomy prospect of a corn crop produced by the ravages of the cut-worm, which were sorely felt the ensuing winter and spring.

Yours truly,   E. F.

Lawrenceburg, June 30, 1851.

LETTER XXVIII.

MR. TORBET—I have not in my recollection any more Indian massacres that occurred in 1792 to record, but there were other difficulties thrown in the way of the new settlements that were almost equally distressing to the inhabitants. After contending with the forests for years, and reclaimed so much that with the same yield of corn they had had in past times they might look for a full supply of bread, and to be reduced by the depredations of the cut-worm one-half, was truly a loss, and severely felt, as the number of the customers was so greatly increased, and the opportunity of obtaining supplies from the fields so much diminished. But these things had to be borne, and very often nettles and pursley (and sometimes without salt or vinegar) had to supply the place of bread and meat. There was, however, one fact that encouraged them, and enabled them to bear up under all these discouragements. There was occasionally a boat load of soldiers arriving (always said to be the forerunners of a numerous army coming on) sufficient to protect all the new settlements. Our information at that time was neither received by lightning or government mails (for we had neither), but by express sent from one military station to another to inform them what was going on, and from the commandants of military posts was communicated, as far as proper, to the people. One of these expresses arrived probably early in July, bringing the gratifying news that Wayne was actually on his march across the mountains with his army on his way to Fort Washington. This news was received with joy, and the arrival of the army expected and waited for with intense anxiety. From the first news of the army having taken up the line of march until it was heard they had gone into winter quarters at Legionville, a short distance below Pittsburg, every ear was open to hear the news from the army, and the time of their expected arrival at Cincinnati was the subject of general conversation; so that for the balance of that and the two succeeding years, Wayne and his army were too intimately connected with the history of the new settlements not to be seen in every page. It was a subject of great regret among the inhabitants that they should have stopped short of Cincinnati, but their confidence in final success was not diminished.

The people were not so much annoyed by Indians during the winters of 1792–3 as they had previously been. Some,

I recollect, assigned as a reason, that they were directing their attention to the headquarters of the army, to ascertain, if possible, Wayne's intended movements, and by what route he would probably invade them.

The spring of 1793 brought with it a calamity unlooked for in the memorable flood of that year. Not knowing the height to which the Ohio had been sometimes swollen, many of the settlers had built their cabins on low ground, where they had made gardens and corn-fields, enclosed with common rail fences. But in April the river rose to such a height that many of them were driven from their places of residence, and had the mortification to see their fences taken off, and in some instances their houses floated down stream with the flood. Fortunately, however the rise in the water was very gradual, and the weather mild, so that they were all able to save what little stock they had. This flood was several feet higher than any that has ever taken place in the Ohio river since, except the floods of '32 and '47.

Soon after the flood had subsided, and the waters were again reduced to their banks, the long looked-for army arrived, making a very formidable appearance as they floated down the Ohio. They passed Columbia on Sunday, I think, about the last of April, but it might have been in the beginning of May. Gen. Wayne and suite first arrived in a keelboat and landed at Columbia, where he probably tarried about an hour, until the fleet came up. He then started in advance of them, passed Cincinnati and took up his headquarters in a beech woods above the mouth of Mill creek, to which he gave the name of Hobson's Choice, by which name it was called for many years, as all the old pioneers of the country can recollect. This event was hailed with joy, and the people now felt as though they were secure.

Yours truly,   E. F.

Lawrenceburg, July 9, 1851.

LETTER XXIX.

MR. TORBET—Soon as it was announced to the new settlements that General Wayne had established his headquarters at Hobson's Choice, and encamped his army on the bank of the Ohio river, between Cincinnati and Mill creek, the anxiety to visit his camp became almost, or quite, universal. Like other boys, I partook of the same feeling, being then ten years of age. It was not long before I gained the consent of my father to accompany a neighbor to the camp, who was going down to sell some vegetables to the soldiers. We descended the river in a small canoe, passed Cincinnati to the east line of the camp, where we were hailed by a sentinel and ordered to land, and questioned what we had on board. The sergeant of the guard was called for, and, on satisfying himself that we had no spirits on board, we were told to pass on to the camp. On landing and ascending the bank of the river, I had before me the most attracting scene I had ever beheld—well calculated to fill with amazement any person, man or boy, who had been four years in the woods, seldom seeing any buildings better than the inferior order of log cabins, except Fort Washington and a few hewed log, and unpainted frame, houses, boarded up on the outside with oak clap-boards from the woods, shaved smooth with the drawing-knife, that were then to be seen in a very scattered condition in Cincinnati. In the encampment there was perfect order. In the first place, the beech trees, which were far the most numerous of any other species, were nearly all of a size and height, spreading out their branches so as to interlock with each other, and form one of the most beautiful arbors I have ever seen, with but very little undergrowth; and what had been there the army had removed as far as the encampment extended—the whole of which, in point of cleanliness, would compare with the door-yards of any of our neat farmers in the present day. In an exact line with the river, and in rows as straight as a line, the whited tents were fitted up in the neatest style, extending, I suppose, at least a half a mile along the river, leaving a space next to the bank of the river about the width of Front street in Cincinnati, and in the same manner rows were formed in the rear of each other, until space enough was occupied for the whole army. In the rear of the encampment there was built a row of shantees by setting posts in the ground and siding up and covering them over with boat-plank, which were used as stables for their horses. Near the center of this encampment, up and down the river, General Wayne had his markee. If I remember right, in the second row from the river, leaving an open space in front, and at the proper places throughout the camp, the markees of the different officers were to be seen—the whole presenting a scenery (taking into consideration the state of the improvements of the country in 1793) more attracting than our most magnificent cities present now. Besides here, so far as human effort was concerned, was to be seen the hope of the country in an army who were destined in another year to drive back our savage foes, to retrieve the character of our past failures in arms, and restore the country to peace. Although it is now fifty-eight years since my first visit to Wayne's camp (as it was then commonly called), the prospect then presented seems as vivid, and the flights of imagination that flashed upon my mind as I looked over the whole scene, as lively as it did on that day.

Yours truly,   E. F.

Lawrenceburg, July 15, 1851.

LETTER XXX.

MR. HIBBEN—Since I suspended some numbers I was addressing to Mr. Torbet, containing reminiscences of the early settlement of the Miami country, I have learned that you have become proprietor and editor of the *Independent Press,* the paper in which they were published. The cause of the suspension having been removed, at the request of a number of your subscribers (by your permission) I purpose to address to you a few more numbers for the same paper.

In the winter of 1792–93 the fact that Gen. Wayne, with his army, had taken up winter quarters near the head of the Ohio river, and would descend in the spring to Cincinnati, encouraged a number of adventurers in Columbia and Cincinnati to venture back in the country to settle lands they had purchased, but had not ventured to settle on through fear of danger from the Indians. It was generally supposed by the inhabitants that soon after the army should arrive the campaign would be carried into the Indian country, and give security to the new settlements. The character that Gen. Wayne had acquired as an officer in the Revolutionary war forbid all idea of another failure, and led to a confident belief that the Indians would be driven back, and compelled to sue for peace. Columbia and Cincinnati, at that time, were crowded with a population that only intended to make these places a temporary residence, who were anxious to remove to their own lands. Col. Israel Ludlow, who had previously commenced an improvement on Mill creek, but on account of its exposedness to danger, had abandoned it for a time, reoccupied it that winter, and three miles higher up the creek Capt. Jacob White, from Columbia, with a few families, settled another station, and still higher up the creek Tucker's and Cunningham's stations were settled. The same winter Mr. John

Beasley erected a large block house near the bank of the Little
Miami, to which he removed his family preparatory to build-
ing a mill at the place (now known as Armstrong's lower
mills). In the spring of 1793 a number of families from
Columbia, Cincinnati and North Bend made a settlement at
the mouth of the Big Miami, which was called the point.
Among the families from Columbia I recollect those of Mr.
Hugh Dunn, Mr. Benjamin Randolph and Mr. Isaac Mills.
In addition to these there was also a settlement made at
Round Bottom, a short distance below Covalt's station and
above Newtown, which had been settled the previous year.
The arrival of Gen. Wayne and army in the spring increased
the confidence of the new settlements, and caused other families to join them. They argued that the presence of so large
an army at Cincinnati would deter the Indians, and keep
them at a distance. But some, who thought they understood
the Indian character better, said they would constantly keep
small parties of their most daring warriors hovering about our
frontiers to watch the movements of the army, and that the
exposed frontiers would be more liable to attacks. With the
last opinion Mr. William Smalley, who had escaped from his
captivity among the Indians, and returned home about Christmas, agreed, he having accompanied Major Trueman, Hardin
and Freeman on their visit to the Indians with a flag of
truce, and witnessed the murder of Major Trueman and his
waiter, and being satisfied that Hardin and Freeman, with
whom they had parted the afternoon before Trueman was
killed, had shared the same fate. Mr. Smalley warned the
people that they would have no abatement of hostilities until
the Indians were whipped. He said they as much expect to
defeat Wayne as they were certain that they had Harmar and
St. Clair. The first circumstance confirming the correctness
of either opinion was an attack on Mr. Beasley's block house.
He employed the time, after removing his family (or rather

his two families, for, having a large family of his own, he had married a Mrs. Prichet, with one equally large, so that the two united could furnish seven good fighting men for defense), in collecting materials for his mill. Among other materials, he had drawn a large pile of stone for a foundation, lying from the river bank back to near the upper corner of the house. One Sunday evening the dogs, of which he had a number, appeared to be very much disturbed, and would frequently move a short distance from the house toward the hill, and bark furiously, which gave suspicions that there were Indians about. The barking of the dogs increased with more fury after dark, and continued through the night. Toward day they appeared frantic, and changed their course toward the pile of stone. On observing the fury of the dogs, Mr. Beasley, as I heard him say the day following, concluded he would venture out into the yard to see if he could make any discoveries. He accordingly opened the door and walked out in a direction toward the river bank, but observing the dogs run towards the pile of stone and jump back, he concluded there might be Indians there, and that he had better return to the house. On turning round, he was alarmed by the report of a gun from behind the stone pile, the ball of which nearly grazed his head. He quickened his speed, and saw a number of Indians running toward the door, as though trying to cut off his retreat. He, however, succeeded in getting there first, and having secured the door with bars, he, with his boys, took their stations at the port holes in the upper part of the house, where they saw the Indians in the woods concealing themselves behind the trees. Mr. Beasley said he noticed one place himself behind a large tree, and immediately pointed his gun through a port hole in a direction toward the tree, waiting an opportunity to shoot; that he soon saw the Indian's head, and his gun pointed at him, and was in the act of shooting, when he received a ball in his right wrist, which for a moment paralyzed his finger, then on the trigger, but that he immediately recovered the shock, and shot and killed the Indian, after which they (the Indians) made no other exertion, only to escape in the safest way they could. When I saw Mr. Beasley, and heard him relate the story, the ball was not yet extracted.

Yours with sincere respect, E. F.

Lawrenceburg, September 15, 1851.

LETTER XXXI.

MR. HIBBEN—After the attack on Mr. Beasley's blockhouse, noticed in my last, with the exception of stealing a few horses, the new settlements were but little disturbed by Indians until near the close of summer. Sometime about the last of August, as Mr. Moses Prior and his brother-in-law, Mr. Goble, were digging some potatoes to take to Wayne's camp, the next morning, to sell to the soldiers, they supposed they heard turkeys calling in the woods on a side hill a little above the place where they were working, and Mr. Goble said he would go and shoot one. About this time, Mrs. Prior had gone to the bank of Mill creek to milk the cows, taking her second child with her, leaving the youngest sleeping in the cradle, the oldest being with his father in the field, which was near by. Mr. Goble had left but a very short time, until Mr. Prior said he heard the report of a gun, and supposed he had shot at a turkey, but as he did not hear any fall concluded he had missed, and commenced working again; but almost instantly turned his eyes in that direction, and saw a number of Indians, armed with guns and tomahawks, rushing out of the woods, making their way with all possible speed towards his house. In the confusion and hurry of the moment, he forgot his little boy, and ran toward the house, but, finding himself cut off from that retreat, he thought of his son, and turned round to try and save him, when he beheld him already in the possession of the Indians. He then retreated across the creek to Captain White's block-house, where he found Mrs. Prior, who had been more fortunate than himself; for, on hearing the alarm, and seeing the Indians already in possession of the house, she seized the little boy she had with her, and plunged into the creek, where the water was up to her shoulders, and made her way with him to the block-house before her husband had arrived there. The Indians entered Prior's house, killed the little child left in the cradle, and destroyed the bedding, and some other property; then crossed over to the west side of the creek, and made a regular attack on the principal station. They took their first stand behind some trees, at what was supposed rather beyond the reach of gun-shot from the block-house; and sent an Indian with the little boy in his arms, held in such a position that would endanger his life if the white people shot at him. In this way he approached within speaking distance, and summoned them to surrender; promising as a condition to spare their lives; but, finding his summons was disregarded, he soon stepped backward, keeping the boy between himself and danger, until, supposing he was beyond the reach of their bullets, he took little Jack by the heels, and, with a swing, beat his head against a tree and killed him. Some person in the block-house who saw him perform this brutal act, shot through a port-hole and killed the Indian. Seeing one of their number fall, the Indians seemed more determined to rescue his dead body than to make any further attempt to take the station. And, approaching from tree to tree, they made a rush, and seized the body of the dead Indian, and commenced bearing it away; but, in the attempt, a second Indian was killed. They, however, succeeded in bearing them both away a short distance, and then disappeared.

As soon as it was supposed they were gone, one of the men at the station started for Cincinnati and Columbia to give the alarm, and ask for assistance; fearing they might return again and renew the attack. Early the next morning they were sufficiently reinforced by the militia from both places, who were always ready to go when called for. Among those who went to their assistance from Cincinnati was Mr. Stephen Ludlow, one of our most enterprising farmers, living, at this time, in the neighborhood of Lawrenceburg, and who is still actively engaged in superintending his farming operations. Mr. Ludlow was the first man who found the bodies of the two Indians killed, where they had been left, in Captain White's corn-field. The militia, in their search, found the remains of Mr. Goble, who had been shot, and of Mr. Prior's two children. This was considered by the white people a very bold attempt on the part of the Indians. To attack White's station, within nine miles of Cincinnati and five of Columbia, with several other stations further advanced into the country, filled the inhabitants of the new settlements with more consternation than any former attempt they had made. But lest I should be too tedious, I will close for the present.

Yours with much respect,   E. F.

Lawrenceburg, September 25, 1851.

———

LETTER XXXII.

MR. HIBBEN—After a long suspension, occasioned by a severe indisposition, which at one time seemed to threaten my life, I now resume the series of letters I promised your readers.

In my last I gave an account of the attack of the Indians on White's station, and the panic it produced in the minds of the inhabitants of the out stations. I will now proceed to an account of a different character, which diffused gladness into the hearts of all the inhabitants of the Miami country, and inspired them with a confidence that their warfare was soon to end. On Sunday morning, September 7, 1793, in pursuance of a general order from the commander-in-chief, the army of General Wayne took up the line of march for the frontiers, and, it was then thought by the people, for an immediate attack on the Indian towns. In their march they passed up the valley of Mill creek, following the trace of General St. Clair's army in their march in 1791, crossing the big Miami at Fort Hamilton. They continued their course, by way of Fort St. Clair, and after a march of seven days, arrived at Fort Jefferson on the 13th, at which place the general made a halt for a short time. But, not being pleased with the location, after a short stay he moved the army six miles north and built another fort, which, in honor of General Green, of the revolutionary army, he called Greenville. At this place the army went into winter quarters, except a regiment (designated the rowdy regiment), which was ordered to encamp on the first high ground on the west bank of the Big Miami, about its junction with the Ohio, to afford protection to keel-boats which might descend the Ohio with supplies for the army, to ascend the Miami up to Fort Hamilton, that being the best way at that time to convey heavy articles from Cincinnati to that place. The above named place of encampment is still known as the rowdy camp in the neighborhood of Lawrenceburg up to the present time. In the latter part of October, General Wayne was reinforced at Greenville by the arrival of General Scott from Kentucky with a thousand mounted militia. But, having determined not to proceed against the Indians until spring, they were sent back and dismissed until that time. During that winter every exertion that could be was made to forward as large an amount of provisions as

possible to the outposts, that the army might not be embarrassed, as St. Clair had been, for the want of full rations.
In December General Wayne sent a detachment from his army
to St. Clair's battle-ground, which they took possession of
on Christmas, and proceeded to erect a fort, which was called
Fort Recovery, affording an opportunity of sending on supplies in advance of the army, so that by spring he had an
abundance for any force he might want to collect on the
frontiers. General Wayne, in all his arrangements, gave evidence that he was not only brave but also prudent and skill-
ful in the discharge of all the duties confided to him, and
gave to the people increased confidence of all final success.

Fearing I shall weary the patience of your readers, I will
close for the present, and subscribe myself
                        Your friend,   E. F.
Lawrenceburg, December 8, 1851.

———

LETTER XXXIII.

MR. HIBBEN—The infant settlements in the Miami country
did not enjoy that repose from Indian alarms and depredations that, from some former circumstances, they had anticipated when the army removed to Greenville. Small parties
of Indians still hovered round the settlements with hostile designs, as the history of their following movements will show.
The first I recollect was the following: Some time toward
the last of October, or beginning of November, Mr. Benjamin Olcott (being a constable) was called on business to
that part of the town of Columbia called the hill, between
which and the river there is a tract of low land subject to frequent inundations of water, so as to prevent any families
from settling on it. On his return home, Mr. Olcott had
to pass through a long, narrow lane, connecting at that time

the two parts of the town, as it was then called.   In traveling home, though about the full of the moon, it was a part of the time very dark, owing to the scuds that frequently obscured the moon.   Mr. Olcott afterwards said that, turning his head around after one of these scuds had passed the moon, he thought he saw an Indian following him.   He felt alarmed, but he thought it would be unsafe for him to make any delay, in order to ascertain the fact, and so he hastened his pace home on horseback.   On riding up to the door (which was but a very short distance from my father's house), he threw his bridle over a stake in the fence, took off his saddle and went into his house, took it up a ladder, and threw it into the loft, as all the upper floors of all their cabins were then called.   He returned to put his horse in the stable, but he was gone.   He said he felt for the stake, thinking he might possibly have slipped the bridle, but it was not there. He had strong suspicions of what had become of his horse, but dare not tell, fearing that he might be wrong and subject himself to the charge of cowardice.

He then returned to the house, and told his wife that his horse had got loose, and gone, and he would let him go until morning. Next morning, being Sabbath morning, search was made in vain for the horse, and after reasonable attempt was made to find him and failed, Mr. Olcott told what he thought he had seen the night before, while passing down the lane, and what he then believed had become of his horse, in which opinion all appeared to concur.   At the usual hour for public worship, the people assembled at the meeting-house, built on the front of the hill by the Baptist church (being the first house built for the worship of God in the Miami country).   About the time for public worship to commence, two men came down the hill with Olcott's horse and an Indian scalp.   The scalp seemed to electrify the congregation, and

22

without attending to the forms of worship most of them made
their way home in the most speedy manner they could. The
two men named had gone to the woods the day before, in
search of some hogs that had wandered off to the woods during the summer in search of food, and, not succeeding, they
wandered about until it was so late they could not find their
way home. On their way home in the morning they saw
the Indian riding the horse (very carelessly as they thought),
and hid behind trees until he nearly approached them, when
they shot and scalped him, and brought the horse and scalp
in with them. The result was, the Indian lost his scalp, the
worship for the day was suspended, and Olcott's horse was
returned to him.   Yours,

(Published Dec. 26, 1851.)   E. F.

LETTER XXXIV.

MR. HIBBEN—Soon after the removal of Wayne's army
from Cincinnati to Greenville, in 1793, the settlements were
visited by a calamity which (as far as human life was concerned) was far more destructive than the Indians had been.
In December the small-pox, in its most malignant form, made
its appearance among them, and spread with such rapidity that
its progress could not be arrested until it had reached the re-
motest station. But this calamity, severe as it was, brought
with it some consolation. Many indulged the hope that the
Indians, in their intrusions, would catch the disease and convey it home, to the destruction of their people there. All
business was suspended, as well as all assembling for public
purposes, or military trainings, and the whole attention of the
people was directed toward finding out the best and most
speedy way of eradicating the disease from the country before spring. Houses most detached, where they could be

had, were selected for pest-houses, and all who were willing to risk the process of inoculation were encouraged to resort to them as speedily as possible, where men were prepared to inoculate them without charge. Among others, the house of Mr. John Smith (pastor of the Baptist church) was selected, it being an entire frontier house, and Mr. S. being a very friendly and benevolent man, great numbers resorted to it.

After the disease had subsided, the families who had used Mr. Smith's house met to assist his family in cleaning up, as they called it. Every part of the house, where it was thought any part of the contagion could have been deposited, was scoured, and all their wearing apparel and bed clothing were washed. To make the cleansing as effectual as possible, the family clothed themselves for the day in old and worn-out garments that had been laid aside, intending to burn them the next day, when they should put on their clean clothes. In order to avail themselves of a white frost expected that night, the whole were left out, and the want of bed and bed clothing made up for through the night by a good warm fire. A family thus situated would of course be like those who are watching for the morning. The reader can judge in part of their surprise when it was announced at the dawn of the day that their clothes were gone. " Gone! where to?" said one in surprise. "We can not tell," was the answer. It was of no use to inquire; they were all gone, and no one would suspect any neighbor for having done it, for they could neither be worn nor concealed without exposure. All that could be learned was that two men, shod with moccasins, had passed along the fence where they were spread out early in the evening. They knew it must have been early, as their feet made deep indentations in the soft ground, which they were certain could not have been done long after dark, as it froze hard at an early hour. Here, for the present, I must leave Mr. Smith and his clothing in rather a bad fix, his neighbors, though they might wish to relieve him, could not for want of means. A few days after, some Indians penetrated the very heart of the settlement of Columbia and stole two horses from the stable of Mr. Thomas Hubble close by his dwelling-house, To reach Mr. Hubble's stable, they had to pass through the settlement, at least about a mile, at a place where I suppose three hundred men, armed and equipped for fight, might have been raised by the sound of a horn in one hour. In addition to other facts there was something more daring in this, from the consideration that they had, with their toma-hawks and scalping knives, to cut away the check of the stable door before they could reach the horses. The alarm was given in the morning as soon as the fact was known, and large numbers assembled to determine what should be done. Mr. Hubble was highly esteemed, and there was a great deal of sympathy for him, but more indignation for so daring an outrage, and determination to punish it. Each of the militia Captains Flinn, Hall and Kibbey, proposed to raise volunteers and follow after, but finally agreed to go together and act in concert. As soon as they had time to fill their sacks with parched corn they were off on the trail of the horses, which it was ascertained had crossed the Miami at Flinn's ford, opposite Turkey bottom, and passed up on the east side of that river. On the second day, Capt. Hall was of the opinion that the prospects were not sufficiently flattering to continue the pursuit and returned. On the third day Capt. Flinn, who was the oldest officer, and considered an excellent woodsman, expressed the opinion that they were risking too much for any probable success they might expect to meet with; but Capt. Kibbey, though he would not oppose Capt. Flinn's opinion, said that if seven others would follow him he would keep up the pursuit another day, whereupon John Clawson, Richard M. Gano, Isaac Ferris, Jr., Thomas McCardle, Sylvanus Reynolds, Benjamin Stites, Jr., and

Ephraim Simpson agreed to follow Capt. Kibbey, and Capt. Flinn and the balance returned home. The next day, being near the Indian town called Old Chillicothe, on the Little Miami, Capt. Kibbey and his men thought it the most prudent to return, accordingly they turned about and followed Harmar's trace home. On the second morning of their return, soon after taking up the line of march, they saw two men at a distance coming towards them on the trace, apparently heavy loaded, and ascertaining that they were Indians they hid behind trees until they came opposite them, when they shot, and killed them both. After scalping them they examined their packs, and found them to contain Mr. Smith's clothes, which, with the Indian scalps, they brought in with them. Capt. Kibbey and his men were very much applauded for this affair, and Mr. Smith proposed to give them ten dollars each for his returned goods, but I believe few, if any, received it.

The goods were uninjured except an attempt to unravel one or two new coverlets to plait bats of woolen yarn, that had been used for filling, it being of various beautiful colors.

Lawrenceburg, Dec. 29.   E. F.

N. B.—I may be mistaken as to two or three of the names of Captain Kibbey's party.

LETTER XXXV.

MR. HIBBEN—The excitement produced by the return of Captain Kibbey's party with Mr. Smith's goods, and the scalp of the Indians who stole them, had not subsided, when the following occurrence took place.

About the time that General Wayne arrived, with his army at Cincinnati, Mr. Henry Tucker removed from Columbia, with several families accompanying, on to Mill creek, and estab-

lished what was then called Tucker's station. Mr. Tucker
had two very valuable horses, which, after the summer was
over, he sent back to Columbia for safe-keeping. Mr.
Tucker had, at Columbia, a very strong stable, from which,
it was thought, the Indians would not be able to steal his
horses, the horses and stable, if I remember right, were placed
in the charge of Mr. Joseph Lambert, and thought to be entirely safe. One morning, about the 1st of April, the alarm
was given that the Indians were about, and that Mr. Tucker's
horses were stolen. Mr. Tucker was sent for, and, in the
meantime, before his arrival, large crowds of the militia had
assembled at the stable, to find out, if possible, how the
stable door was opened. Mr. Tucker, on his arrival, offered
a reward of eighty dollars for the return of the horses, and
the militia were soon off on the pursuit of them. They had
no difficulty in keeping the track of the horses and Indians
through the day; so that they could follow on as fast as their
strength and activity would permit, but at night the Indians
had the advantage. They could make tracks, but the white
people could not follow them until morning, and, had they im-
proved the opportunity, might easily have escaped. Directly
after starting on the track the second morning, some of the
white men discovered a smoke ahead, which they soon learned
was an Indian camp. An arrangement was made to approach it with all possible caution, but the Indians were too
vigilant. One of them saw the white people coming, and gave
the yell, when they all broke for the woods but one, who,
being a little more resolute than the rest, made for the horses,
and, with his scalping knife, cut the rope with which they
were tied fast to a tree and made an attempt to mount one
of them, but they were very tall and he failed. He next
tried to shelter himself between the horses, but, finding the
white men were pressing too hard on him, he took to his
heels and made his escape, although several guns were shot

at him, and most of the white men believed he was wounded, but thought it more prudent to return with the recaptured horses than to risk anything further in pursuing after the Indians. Thus, after an absence of four days, Mr. Tucker's horses were returned to him at an expense of eighty dollars, and the Indians taught that they could not longer, with impunity, intrude on the property of the white people.

Yours,   E. F.

Lawrenceburg, Jan. 5.

LETTER XXXVI.

MR. HIBBEN—The depredations of the Indians on the inhabitants of the Miami country in the winter of 1793–94 were not confined to the settlement of Columbia, but other stations were made to share in the evil. In the spring of 1793, as related in a former letter, a number of families from Columbia and other places made a settlement on the east side of the Big Miami, a little above its junction with the Ohio, near a place called the Goose Pond. During that season a Mr. Rittenhouse built a mill to grind corn on a small stream passing down the hill to the Miami, through where the town of Cleves now stands. The mill was a wet weather concern, the stream being small; but it was a great accommodation to the people at that time. In the after part of the winter, or beginning of spring, after a rain sufficient to supply the mill with water, a Mr. Demos, with a young man by the name of Micajah Dunn, and another young man whose name I can not recollect, went from the settlement before named to Mr. Rittenhouse's mill, with each a bag of corn to have it ground into meal, and were detained so as not to start home until after dark; that, however, produced but little inconvenience, as it was very bright moonlight. A short distance after leaving the mill they came to the residence of a Mr. Wheeling; and, seeing several persons there, Mr. Dunn and the other young man with him rode up to the door to make some inquiry, but Mr. Demos rode on, expecting soon to be overtaken by them. While sitting on their horses talking at the door (as they supposed about twenty minutes after Mr. Demos left them), they heard a firing of guns in the direction he had gone; that, however, created no great alarm, as the white people were in the habit of going out such moonlight nights to kill wild game. They immediately started on hearing the guns, and, after riding as briskly as their horses could well travel with the load they had to carry, about the distance to where they supposed the firing was, they found Mr. Dennis lying across the path dead, and the bag of meal by his side. It would be useless to attempt to describe their feelings in that trying moment, traveling a narrow path in the woods, surrounded by a large growth of trees, behind which they might easily imagine their enemies were concealed, ready to shoot at them the fatal balls by which their leader had just been shot down, without means of defense and not knowing whether by advancing or retreating they would be exposed to the most dangers. Their course was onward, and proved to be a safe one, for they reached their home, gave the alarm, and a party was roused to go out after, and convey, the corpse of Mr. Demos to his family. who, instead of returning with his bag of meal, as was expected, to supply their daily wants, was brought in a mangled, lifeless corpse, that they might behold him once more, take a last farewell view, then commit him to the silent grave, to be seen by them on earth no more. The bloody scene above narrated took place almost within the hearing of the guns at Lawrenceburg, had there been any person there to have heard, a remembrance of which presents to the mind a wide contrast from the state of things as they now exist.

Who that is not void of feeling can reflect on the sufferings that have been endured, on the labors, toils and sweat, the dangers and untimely deaths that have been passed through, to provide in this goodly land for those who might follow after a peaceful home, surrounded more abundantly with all the necessary articles of life, probably than any other country in the world has ever been blessed with, without feeling his heart swell with emotions of gratitude at the remembrance of the names of those early pioneers, who had abandoned all the charms connected with their former peaceful homes, and sundered all the delightful ties that bound them to their former associations that posterity might enjoy the blessings procured for them at so great a cost. The Mr. Dunn above alluded to was the oldest brother of Judge Isaac Dunn, now living in this place, and the father of a respectable family raised in our country, most of whom are still among us.

Lawrenceburg, Jan. 15.   E. F.

LETTER XXXVII.

MR. HIBBEN—In my last three letters, I tried to show the dangerous situation the citizens of the Miami country were placed in by reciting several hostile acts committed by the Indians on individuals, in person, and on their private property. I now invite your attention back to the movements of the army; which was the all-important topic of conversation in that day. The transfer of the army, and of General Wayne's headquarters, from Hobson's Choice to Greenville, made a great change in the business of the country. The latter place became the resort of those who were seeking a market for the little amount of surplus produce they had to spare, and the track opened by General St. Clair, which had previously been used only as a military road, became a great thoroughfare, thronged by citizens and soldiers, going to and from head-quarters. The change gave the Indians an opportunity to waylay the road and kill and plunder as circumstances would permit, and though generally escorted by detachments of soldiers they were frequently attacked and plundered. Among the number killed was Mr. Moses Pryor, who had lost two children killed by the Indians at the time they attacked White's Station, leaving Mrs. Pryor, with one little boy she had saved by her own exertions at the time, to mourn his loss, and that little fellow fell a victim to fever the next fall, so that she was, indeed, a lonely, forlorn widow, far away from her relatives and former associates, left to buffet alone the storms of adversity with which she had been so often assailed.

Colonel Robert Elliott (attached to the army) was another victim to savage barbarity. He was traveling on horseback (in company with a soldier who served him as waiter) from Cincinnati to Fort Hamilton, and at a place then called the Big Hill, in Springfield township, was fired on and killed by the Indians. The soldier escaped, followed by Colonel Elliott's horse, and made his way to Fort Hamilton. The next day a party was raised (and a coffin provided), who went with the soldier to the spot, and found the body of Colonel Elliott, placed it in the coffin, and started to Cincinnati to bury it. They had traveled but a short distance before they were attacked by the Indians, by whom the soldier was killed, and the coffin, with the remains of Colonel Elliott, taken. In a very short time the white people rallied, and re-took the body of Colonel Elliott, with his waiter, and proceeded with them to Cincinnati, where they were buried the next day.

The spring opened with an encouraging prospect of an early, vigorous, and successful campaign, and rumors were continually afloat of boats loaded with soldiers, descending the river to Fort Washington, and making their way from that place to headquarters. A company of spies were called for from Columbia, which was soon raised, and organized by the appointment of Ephraim Kibbey, captain, William Brown, lieutenant, and Ashbel Gray, ensign, and ordered to march with all possible dispatch for headquarters. While contemplating the pleasing prospect before them, with a glowing delight, an express arrived from the army, bringing news of a most unpleasant character. General Wayne had been using every possible exertion, through the winter and spring, to get as large an amount of supplies on to the frontiers as possible, and had, in the latter part of June, ordered between two and three hundred horses (loaded I suppose) on from Greenville to Fort Recovery, and had detached one hundred and forty men under the command of Major McMahen, to escort them. The major arrived at Fort Recovery on the evening of the 29th, and it may be supposed the supplies forwarded were deposited in the fort, but the place being too small to hold the horses, and it being desirable to let them graze as a matter of economy, the escort encamped outside the fort. Early on the morning of the 30th they were attacked by an overwhelming force of Indians, and, after a brave and desperate struggle, Major McMahen, Captain Hartshorn, Lieutenant Craig and Ensign Torry having been slain, and fifty-one privates killed, wounded and missing, they were compelled to retire into the fort, abandoning their horses to the victors, who hung about through the day, and made several ineffectual attempts to storm the fort; but, seeming a little modest about pressing the matter too far, they, in the course of the following night, retired with the horses they had captured. News of the above misfortune hung like a dark cloud over the mind for a few days, but it soon passed off. The people had too much confidence in Wayne to be shaken by one adverse wind, and the circumstance was almost forgotten in a

short time by the joy that was felt on the arrival of General
Scott, from Kentucky, with sixteen hundred mounted volunteers, who passed immediately on for headquarters, where they
arrived on the 26th of July, and were reported to Wayne, at
which time he announced himself ready to march in search of
the enemy. Here I will come to a close, after expressing my
regret that I should, when writing my last letter, have forgotten the name of Thomas Fuller, the young man who was
with Micajah Dunn at the time Mr. Demos was killed by the
Indians.   E. F.

Lawrenceburg, January 19, 1852.

N. B.—The reader will please read Demos for Dennis in
my last letter.

LETTER XXXVIII.

MR. HIBBEN—On the 28th of July, 1794, Major-General
Anthony Wayne was in command of an army of efficient,
well-disciplined, brave men, powerful enough in numbers to
have awed the Indians into submission, had it not been for
the folly of their advisers. The army numbered (as was
generally understood) over five thousand effective men,
equipped for war, well supplied with military stores and provisions, the larger portion of them regulars, divided into two
brigades—one under the command of Brigadier-General
James Wilkinson, the other commanded by Brigadier-General
Thomas Posey; the militia were under the command of Major-General Scott. This army, through the persevering, un-
tiring industry of General Wayne, had been drilled until it is
probable the United States never had had together at one
time an equal force of brave men, better disciplined and prepared for action. Thus prepared, with Captains Debutts and
Lewis, and Lieutenant William Henry Harrison for his aids-

de-camp, Wayne moved with his army, on the 28th of July,
in search of the enemy, and, from reports circulated among
the people, was equally cautious, as he had been on his
march to Greenville, to have his camp well guarded, so that
there was no night on his march in which he could have been
attacked by surprise. After leaving Fort Recovery, about
twenty-four miles in his rear, he built another fort, which he
called Fort Adams. From Fort Adams he directed his
course toward the junction of the Maumee and Auglaize,
where it was expected the Indians would make a stand, but
being disappointed in this (as they all fled at his approach)
he made another halt of several days and erected another
fort, which he called Fort Defiance. From Fort Defiance he
crossed over the Maumee, and marched down the course of
that river on its left bank towards the rapids, and on the 18th
lost one of his spies (William May), taken prisoner by the
enemy. On the 19th, believing the Indians were so closely
pursued that they would either come to a fight or disperse,
Wayne had another fort erected, called Fort Deposit. In
this fort he ordered the heavy baggage that it would be inconvenient to be encumbered with in time of an action to be
deposited, leaving a sufficient force to protect it. The next
morning (August 20th) at an early hour the army was put
in motion in search of the enemy, prior to which the commander-in-chief issued a general order directing the manner
of conducting. They had not moved far before they had
sufficient indications of an intention on the part of the Indians to join issue with them, and to prepare for the conflict.
Every necessary arrangement was made that could be made
while on their march, so that they should not be surprised or
thrown into confusion whenever the attack should be commenced; that is, they were prepared for the engagement at
any time the enemy might choose to make the attack. They
moved on until approaching some fallen timber calculated to

obstruct their march; an advanced corps of mounted men were fired on from a thicket of undergrowth, and driven back to the advanced line of the regular troops, which soon brought on an engagement with as large a portion of our army as the nature of the ground would admit of. The Indians kept up a very brisk fire for some time, but finding the battle to be rather hot they gave way and began to fall back, closely pursued by our men, until they came to an open space, when they dispersed and fled in every direction, many of them toward the British fort, followed by our army until it was seen they received no protection from the garrison, when they gave up the pursuit. Thus in the space of an hour, or probably less, a victory almost bloodless (compared with some of the first engagements) was obtained over the combined forces of the Indian tribes, a victory as important to the interests of the west as was that gained by Washington at Yorktown over the forces of Great Britain under Lord Cornwallis to the united colonies. When the news of this victory reached the settlements, to use a common expression, it spread almost with the rapidity of lightning, and to judge of its effects in Columbia, diffused universal joy into all minds throughout every station then settled. The people were almost frantic with joy, and the first thing heard when they met was congratulations on account of the late triumph of our arms over the savages. To a people, many of whom the last five or six years had been penned up in a small fort, or the more circumscribed limits of a log cabin, beyond which they could not go but at the risk of life, whose last act when they retired to rest at night was to see that every avenue by which their dwelling might be entered was sufficiently barred to prevent the entrance of the midnight assassin, with his tomahawk and scalping knife, from breaking in to execute his murderous intentions, to be at once relieved of all apprehensions of danger, so that they could repose in safety at home, and without fear attend to their business abroad, it was indeed transporting, and calculated to call into lively éxercise every emotion of gratitude and joy hitherto latent in the breast. The length of my letter admonishes me to close.

Yours with respect,   E. F.

Lawrenceburg, January, 1852.

———

LETTER XXXIX.

MR. HIBBEN—After the victory obtained by the United States army, commanded by General Wayne, on the 20th of August, 1794, the commander observed the same prudence and manifested equal skill as before the battle. As it had been understood from various rumors that the Indians were daily in expectation of reinforcements, Wayne remained on the battle-ground three days to await a second attack, should they be disposed to another engagement. At the close of three days, no enemy appearing, he conducted his victorious army back to Fort Defiance, at which place he remained two or three weeks to strengthen his works there, when he removed to the Miami village, near where the town of Fort Wayne now stands, to select the site for another fort in the heart of the Indian country, in which he determined to leave a sufficient force to check any hostile movements of the enemy in the bud. After having determined on the situation and the plan of the fort intended to be erected, he left the prosecution of the work in the charge of one of his officers, Colonel Hamtramck, and removed with the main body of the army back to Greenville, where he again established his headquarters, having previously ordered the militia back to Fort Washington to be discharged and mustered out of service. On their return, every portion of the army, and every individual who had belonged to it, was cheered in the most enthusiastic manner by the citizens, and to have belonged to Wayne's army was enough to elevate any individual (in the estimation of the people) almost to the pinnacle of fame. The officer to whom the erection of the fortification was committed, after having performed the work, named it Fort Wayne. During the winter, preliminaries of peace were signed by General Wayne and the chiefs of the principal tribes, and an arrangement made to hold a treaty at Greenville the ensuing spring to establish a definite and lasting treaty of peace. By the preliminary arrangement both parties were to cease all acts of hostility towards each other, and all prisoners held by either parties were to be delivered up as soon as practicable. The anticipation of peace expressed by the people on hearing of the victory of the 20th of August now began to be realized; the howling of the wolf or the hooting of the owl could no longer be in imagination turned into human voices imitating those animals as an artifice, by which the Indian, unsuspected, could approach the dwelling of the white man from the different points where he had stationed his forces, so as to make a simultaneous attack on every side and cut off all opportunities for a retreat. The writer of this article has often known whole neighborhoods terrified at the report of some one who supposed he had heard the Indians imitating the sound of one or both the animals above named, begun at one point and answered from another, until at about an equal distance from every surrounding point the token was given to move forward and commence the attack, and, as a living witness, can testify that the distress produced on the mind for the time is equally as terrifying as if the danger were near. He remembers (no doubt in common with hundreds of others) often to have lain down at night with the impression deep upon his mind that the probabilities were stronger that before morning he should be a victim of savage cruelty than that he should live to see the light of another day. Can it then be thought a matter of surprise that persons so long suffering so many dangers, privations and fears should be a little enthusiastic in the praise of their deliverers, almost bordering on man worship? I sometimes feel to the present time, when I look over the dangers of past days (old as I am), as though I could throw my hat in the air and raise a hurrah in honor of Wayne and his victorious army, more fortunate, but possibly not more patriotic, than those who had gone before them. But after all, I must say to God be the praise, and to them the honor of being employed by him to bring about so glorious a result. E. F.

Lawrenceburg, February 6, 1852.

LETTER XL.

MR. HIBBEN—The citizens of the Miami country did not realize that exemption from difficulties and dangers on account of Indian depredations at as early a period as they had anticipated; after the victory of the 20th of August, several persons were killed, and other damage accrued in the course of the fall and winter; but it was generally believed that it was the acts of marauding parties, who were out from home and did not know of the truce that had been agreed upon between the hostile parties. The first person killed by the Indians about Columbia, after the battle, that I recollect of, was David Gennings. The circumstances connected with his death by the Indians were so very remarkable that I would not publish them to the world as facts were I not personally acquainted with Mr. Gennings and many of the circumstances, as to leave no doubt, in my own mind, that all I am about to relate to you is true. Mr. Gennings was a respectable farmer, living in Fayette county, Pennsylvania, near where the town

23

of Brownsville now stands, then called Red Stone Old Fort, and in the neighborhood from which Major Benjamin Stites and his party emigrated in 1788, when they descended the river to make the first settlement ever made by the white people in the Miami country. Having heard of the arrival of Major Stites and party, and of their success in making their settlement before they were discovered by the Indians, and of the extraordinary fertility of the soil, Mr. Gennings determined to move his family to Columbia in the spring of 1790, and accordingly made the necessary preparations the preceding winter. At the time he made his arrangements to start, he had had all his effects that he intended to take, except such as were wanted for their comfort in cooking and sleeping the last night, placed in the boat the previous day, so as to make an early start the next morning. In the night he dreamed he had performed his trip down the river in safety, but, after arriving at Columbia, had been most horribly killed and mangled by the Indians. He awoke from sleep and told Mrs. Gennings his dream, and appeared, as she said, very much disturbed, and in the morning told her he had concluded to abandon his intention of removing to the Miamies. Mrs. Genning, being a very resolute woman, told him it would be folly in the extreme to abandon the idea of removal on account of a dream, after they had sold their farm, and other property, but all to no purpose, for the more he thought of his dream the greater his reluctance to remove. Finally, finding she could not remove his difficulties by anything she could say, she addressed him thus: "Well, David, if you think you can not with safety go, do you stay here and make another crop, and I and the boys will go to the Miami country, and raise one, and we shall be able to leave if there is danger, and will send you word, and, after hearing from us, if you think you can venture you can follow the next season." The last proposition was agreed to, Mrs.

Gennings, with the family, descended the river, having three sons young men, and Mr. Gennings following in the winter of '90 or '91. After arriving in the country Mr. Gennings was very unhappy on account of his dream, and frequently said to those he talked with upon the subject, that he had no other expectation but that the Indians would kill him. I recollect hearing him express himself, in a conversation with my father, that he expected to be killed by the Indians, and being a very pious Christian he spoke of not being so much terrified at the thought of dying as he was of the cruel, barbarous manner he expected to die. My father then said to him, " If I were in your situation I would take the advice your friends are giving you, to go back to the old settlements, and stay until the Indians are driven back, or make peace." He finally concluded to adopt that course, and made preparations to return to Pennsylvania with a party that expected shortly to start through the wilderness for Wheeling, but when the time to start came he shrank back, fearing he would be killed on the way. He afterwards, apparently with less fear, continued in the country until after Wayne's victory, when he, with most others, thought there was but little more fear from the Indians. Sometime near the 1st of October (breadstuff being very scarce) he gathered a grist of corn and started with it to Round Bottom, to mill, and to avoid danger, if there was any, he crossed the Miami and went through Newtown, and continued his course undisturbed, until he had nearly approached the ford, where he expected to cross the river again, to get over to the mill. As he was passing a grove of papaw bushes he was fired at by two Indians; the ball shot by one of them passed through one lobe of his lungs, but he did not fall, and the horse turned immediately round, and conveyed him home unconscious of much danger; he saw the Indians fly in much haste, instead of following him. After he had arrived at home, though his wound was not considered dangerous, the family and neighbors thought it best to send to Cincinnati for a doctor (for there was none in Columbia). The physician came (I believe Dr. Sellman), and, on examination, told them the wound would prove fatal; he said the ball had passed through his lungs, as was evidenced by the breath passing through the wound as often as he breathed. In the course of the night an inflammation took place, and the next morning he died.

In the confident belief of entering into glory, his death produced a deep sensation upon the minds of those who had often heard him talk of apprehended danger. He was buried in the burying ground attached to the Baptist meeting-house on the hill at Columbia, where, no doubt, his ashes still repose. The funeral sermon was delivered by Elder John Smith, pastor of the church to which he belonged, and was attended by a very large concourse of people, who appeared to feel that a strange, mysterious Providence was connected with the whole affair.

Yours with much respect,   E. F.

Published Feb. 20, 1852.

LETTER XLI.

MR. HIBBEN—The confidence reposed by the people, generally, in General Wayne's ability to subdue or bring the Indians to terms of peace drew a large emigration to the Miami country, during the winter of 1793–94, and the ensuing spring. With the new emigrants, the old settlers, as on former occasions, were willing to divide, as long as they had any provisions, so that before the close of spring corn became very scarce. Of meat they had none but what was taken from the woods. In consequence of the scarcity of corn the people sowed oats as a substitute for corn and hay, and as soon as it sprang up, and grew to a sufficient height, cut it as food for their horses, and other stock used in raising another crop. All other stock not kept at labor, including swine, had to depend on the woods, as their owners had nothing to give them for food. The oats, although a poor substitute, green as they were, were made to answer their purpose until their corn was laid by. Columbia at that time contained a large population, and nearly all the land was cleared and fenced, and nearly all planted, and in corn. The streets were so bare that there was no chance for grazing short of the woods, to which their stock had to go for self-preservation, where many of them met with an untimely death by the wolves and bears. After the new corn had ripened so as to answer for food for hogs, probably about the beginning of November, Mr. Paul and his son, and Mr. Robert Giffen, whose hogs had strayed off during the summer, concluded to go to the woods in search of them, and, according to agreement, started next morning, traveling up the valleys until they passed Turkey bottom, and came to Duck creek, when they took up the creek, and spent most of the day in unsuccessful search after their hogs. Despairing of success, in the after part of the day they undertook to retrace their steps, and make their way home, returning down the creek, nearly on the track they had made in the morning. In traveling home they came near to a large sycamore tree which immediately above the ground had divided into three branches, which had grown to a very large size. Behind this tree, although unperceived by them, was a party of Indians concealed, and immediately after passing it they were fired at, and Robert Giffen and young Paul fell, being shot, and, it was supposed, died immediately. Old Mr. Paul escaped unharmed, and brought in the unfortunate news, which produced a great alarm. The militia, on hearing the news, repaired to the spot, and brought the dead bodies in to their friends.

This melancholy event, following so soon after the death of Mr. Gennings, shook the faith of many about the prospect of a speedy peace, and, the last murder committed by the Indians about Columbia, it kept the people for a long time in a state of alarm.   Connected with the above account are some facts calculated to show the uncertainty of all schemes however well they may be planned.   Mr. Robert Giffen came to the country in advance of his father to raise a crop for his family use when they might arrive.   This was a prudent measure, which all wise men would approve of.   Robert Giffen thought it best to raise a few hogs that they might have meat as well as bread when they might arrive.   This was also wise management, but wise as it was to human view, it was the very means of producing in the family one of the sorest trials they could have been afflicted with, filling every heart with anguish.   If Robert had not come to the country in advance of his father he would not have had any stock to stray off, and draw him to the woods in search of them, and if he had not gone to the woods on that day he would not have been exposed to the fire of the Indians, so that prudent and well arranged as his plans were, they resulted in an evil which, above all others, he would have wished to avoid; thus, being sent for good, the whole plan resulted in evil, showing how weak, and what short-sighted, frail mortals we are.

Yours,   E. F.

Published Feb. 25, 1852.

LETTER XLII.

MR. EDITOR—When in the state that nature had formed it, and before it had been subdued by the hand of man, the big bottom had, in addition to the common trees of the forest, including the thickets of plumb and haw trees, a very luxuriant growth in a vegetable sometimes called the hog-weed, but commonly the horse-weed. This weed was thick on the ground, and in a few weeks in the summer would grow to the height of from ten to fifteen feet, bearing a seed which, when ripe, was eaten by hogs. Soon after the settlement was made by the white people, on the east side of the Big Miami (at the point), some of their hogs crossed over the river to graze and feed in these thickets, and some of them remained so long that no one continued to exercise ownership over them or their increase, until, like the deer in the woods, they became the property of any person who could find and take them. Late in the fall of 1794,[1] several persons from the settlement on the east side of the river crossed over into the bottoms in search of hogs, to use as meat for the ensuing season. Among them were Isaac Mills, Isaac Dunn, Benjamin Cox, Thomas Walters, Joseph Randolph, Joseph Kitchel and Garret Vanness. After an unsuccessful search for the most of the day, it was proposed by some of them to return home for the night and renew the search the next morning; but Cox and Walters thought it would be best to encamp on the ground, so as to have the advantage of an early start in the morning. The balance, disagreeing with them, returned home, and they stayed in the woods. After circumstances made it appear that after the others were gone they followed Double Lick Run down about a hundred yards below the place where the road from Lawrenceburg to Elizabethtown crosses it, when they selected a place to stay for the night, and made a fire to sleep by on the ground. Toward midnight the people at the settlement were very much alarmed at the report of several guns heard in the direction that Cox and Walters were left by the company, and entertained strong fears about their safety, but could not go for their relief until morning.

[1] NOTE—This date is erroneous. The tragedy occurred February 2, 1795. See Centinel of the Northwest Territory, February 7, 1795.

Early next morning a number of persons started to ascertain
the fate of these men. They repaired to the place where
they were when the company left them the last evening, but
not finding them there they scattered through the woods in
search of them, and in a very short time Mr. Garret Vanness and Mr. Isaac Dunn, who were following down the
creek, came upon the body of Mr. Cox by the side of the
place where they had built a fire to sleep by. He had been
shot and scalped and otherwise mangled. The balance of
the company were called together, and after a little search
found Mr. Walters dead in the weeds, seventy or eighty rods
from where he was first shot, and from the appearance of
things concluded he had been first wounded and made an attempt to escape, but was followed, killed and scalped. These
bodies presented a horrible appearance, and though they
were the last persons killed in the Miami country, the barbarity of the savages exercised on them gave but little evidence of a disposition on their part to make peace. The
traveler, passing from Lawrenceburg to Elizabethtown,
as he crosses the run near the stone building lately the residence of the late Thomas Miller, may at any time, by turning his head to the right, glance his eye over the spot where
Benjamin Cox and Thomas Walters, the last victims of savage barbarity in the war, closing with Wayne's treaty, were
cruelly murdered.   Yours,   E. F.

Published March 3, 1852.

LETTER XLIII.

Mr. Editor—I now proceed to give an account of the
last act of hostility committed by the Indians on any of the
inhabitants of the Miami country, coming within the reach of
my recollection. There was formerly a large white (or as it

is sometimes called) water elm tree, standing on the north side of a path leading from Columbia to Cincinnati, through the woods and along the bank of the river. The roots of this tree were of a peculiar growth, rising above the ground, as they spread out from the trunk of the tree, sometimes to the height of six or seven feet, uniting at the top with the body of the tree, and forming a shelter for man or beast in time of a storm. There was on the back or north side of the tree one of those open cells, formed by nature, of an unusual size.

Sometime late in the autumn of 1794, Mr. Reason Baily, one of the first company that landed at Columbia, 1794, to make a settlement there, was traveling on foot from Cincinnati to Columbia, and as he was passing the tree he was seized by three Indians, one taking him by the coat collar, and one by each arm, and led away about five miles north, to an Indian encampment on Harmar's trace, where, he supposed, there were about thirty Indian warriors. After arriving at the camp, an Indian who could talk English began to inquire of him about the military strength of Columbia; to which he replied that he did not know how strong they were, that he was a stranger, and had only lately come there. As he uttered the last words the Indian stared him in the face and pronounced what he said "a lie," and said: "I saw you there when the white people first came to Columbia;" to which Baily replied, "It is true I was there, but have been away and just returned." "That may be," rejoined the Indian. Baily was then ordered to strip himself, and commenced by taking off his coat and handing it to an Indian, two Indians still holding on to their grip of him, one, after his coat was off, to the collar of his shirt, and the other to one arm, leaving an arm loose. He was then ordered to lay off his vest, which he said he threw over his shoulders, and then, making a stop, put his loose hand in his pocket, pretending to take something from it, and hand it to the Indian holding him by the arm, who immediately let go his hold of the arm to receive the thing offered him, at which moment Baily sprang with so much force as to leave his shirt collar with the other Indian and escaped. One Indian followed immediately after, the others stopping to arm themselves. After running a few hundred feet the Indian caught Baily, and a struggle ensued, in which they both came to the ground; while struggling the Indian attempted to draw Baily's knife he had belted around him, from the scabbard, but getting hold too low Baily grabbed the handle above his hand, and, drawing it out, supposed he had cut the Indian, who gave a yell, shook his hand and let go. Baily took the advantage for flight, but by this time found the other two were close at his heels, but, it being dark, the Indians had to stop and listen for the noise he made in the fallen leaves while running, to learn which way he was winding his course, which gave him the advantage. Having gained considerably on them, and being very much exhausted, passing through a very heavy, dark piece of woods, he stopped suddenly, and hugged closely to a tree, and the Indians passed him. After they had gone, as he supposed, about eighty steps beyond him, they stopped about a minute to listen, and then started again in the pursuit. Mr. Baily continued stationary, and in about half an hour heard the Indians returning; as they passed within about two rods of him, heard them talking as though very much displeased, and neither heard or saw them more. After he felt satisfied the Indians were gone, he moved very cautiously for home, but could not stir without making a noise among the leaves of the trees that had fallen to the ground. He, however, succeeded in arriving safe at the frontier house of Mr. John Smith, where he knocked for admittance, but was refused until he told his name and the cause of his calling at that time of night. On telling them he had been taken captive by the Indians, and had escaped, they caught the idea that he was still a prisoner, and that the Indians were using him for the purpose of getting into the house and charged it upon him, but he affirmed so positively that it was not so that they finally let him in.

This act closed the hostile scenes of a six years' sanguinary war that the early pioneers of the Miami country had to wade through, while contending with the forests, to reclaim and bring them into subjection for the use of man.

Yours,   E. F.

Published March 24, 1852.

LETTER XLIV.

MR. EDITOR—In my last letter I gave an account of the closing hostile scene of a six years' bloody war the early settlers of the Miami country passed through, with all the evils attending such a savage warfare, viz.: a continual fear of danger, producing disquietude, frequent alarm, bloodshed, murders, widows and orphans, with penury and want, followed by a state of peace, connecting with it freedom from alarm, domestic security, ease and contentment, health and prosperity, with a fair prospect of an abundant supply of all the comforts of life, with increasing motives to industry, inviting emigration in an earnest ratio and introducing a new era in the history of the country. The prospect of peace engrossed the attention of all, and was the subject of general conversation, and many of the pioneers, as well as late emigrants and strangers from all parts of the United States, were engaged in making preparation to attend the treaty of Greenville the approaching summer. At the appointed time the parties met, a treaty of peace was concluded, signed, approved and published, and all apprehension of further danger put to rest. The joy on receiving the news of peace was universal, and from that time the inhabitants began to scatter over the face of the country. New villages and farms seemed to be brought into existence as by magic, so that the traveler might pass over a district of country and find it an unbroken wilderness, and in a few months repass and find in almost every direction the big work of opening a farm or building up a village, or a town commenced; and such was the progress in improvements and prosperity that, with the exception of a scarcity of bread for a few years, owing to the rapid increase of emigration, and the great amount of labor necessary to open new farms, no country in the world can boast of an equal increase in all the substantial articles necessary for the comfort of man, nor is there a spot on earth where the inhabitants are more secure from danger of being attacked by foreign foe. There, six years after entering the country in pursuit of a future home, the little band of pioneers had found themselves delivered from the fear of their savage foes, with the bright prospect of permanent peace, and a certainty of soon realizing more than their most extravagant imaginations had ever calculated upon. When I attempt to retrospect the events that have passed under my own observation since I landed at Columbia, on the 12th day of December, 1789, and call to mind the situation of the country at that time, then cast my eyes abroad over the same region and see what it is now, I am lost in astonishment, and feel that every attempt to limit the capacity of man to achieve whatever he, in the exercise of reason, may undertake, is severely rebuked, except the power of omnipotence should obstruct his progress.

　　　　　Yours with much respect,　　　　　E. F.
Published March 31, 1852.

www.ingramcontent.com/pod-product-compliance
Lightning Source LLC
Chambersburg PA
CBHW020759020726
47495CB00008B/2498

* 9 7 8 3 7 4 2 8 2 5 1 9 3 *